PTATH

"Stranger, what is your name?"

His name? Why, Ptath, of course. Ptath of Gonwonlane. He felt astounded that the question should have been asked at all. My lord was yelling something about arrows; and simultaneously, there was a poignant pain in Ptath's chest.

He looked down and was amazed to see a thin piece of wood protruding from his left breast. He pulled it out and threw it on the ground. The pain vanished. A second arrow pinned his arm to his body. He tore that out too; and heard a woman cry out:

"Don't you see? *'He whose strength is unlimited, who tires not, and knows no fear . . .'*"

The man's voice lashed out: "What madness are you talking? That's a myth we keep alive for the masses. We've agreed a thousand times that the Goddess Ineznia uses the name Ptath as propaganda." He broke off: *"Why, it's impossible!"*

THE BOOK OF PTATH

by A.E. Van Vogt

DAW BOOKS, INC.
DONALD A. WOLLHEIM, PUBLISHER

1633 Broadway, New York, NY 10019

First DAW Printing, May 1984.

1 2 3 4 5 6 7 8 9

DAW TRADEMARK REGISTERED
U.S. PAT. OFF. MARCA
REGISTRADA. HECHO EN U.S.A.

PRINTED IN U.S.A.

CONTENTS

CHAPTER I

The Return of
Ptath

HE WAS PTATH. NOT THAT HE THOUGHT OF HIS NAME. IT WAS simply there, a part of him, like his body and his arms and legs, like the ground over which he walked. No, that last was wrong. The ground was not of him. There was a relation, of course, but it was a little puzzling. He was Ptath, and he was walking on ground, walking on Ptath. Returning to the city of Ptath, capital of his empire of Gonwonlane after a long absence.

That much was clear, accepted without thought, and it was important. He felt the urgency of it in the way he kept quickening his pace to see whether the next bend of the river would make it possible for him to turn westward.

To the west was a vast spread of grass, trees and blue-misted hills, and somewhere beyond the hills, his destination. With annoyance, he stared down at the river that barred his way. It had kept winding, twisting back on itself, forcing him time and again to retrace his footsteps. At first that hadn't seemed to matter. Now it did. With all his heart and all his dim consciousness, he longed to be rushing toward those western hills, laughing, shouting in his glee for what he would find there.

Just what he would find wasn't completely certain. He was Ptath, returning to his people. What were those people like? What was Gonwonlane like? He couldn't remember. He strained for the answer that seemed to quiver just beyond reach of his consciousness.

He must cross the river, that much he knew. Twice he stepped down into the shallow wetness nearest shore; and each time drew back, repelled by the alienness. The problem brought the first pain of purposeful thought that he had known since he came out of blackness. In bewilderment he turned his gaze to the hills that lay low on the horizon to the south, and east, and north. They looked the same as the hills to the west, with one vital difference: *He* wasn't interested in them.

He brought his gaze back to the western hills. He had to go to them, river or no river. Nothing could stop him. The purpose was like a wind, a storm that raged inside him. Across the river, a world of glory beckoned. He stepped down into the water, shrank back momentarily, then waded into the dark, swirling current. The river tugged at him, and it seemed to be alive like himself. It, too, moved over the land, and was not a part of the land.

His thought ended as he stepped into a deep hole. The water crowded hungrily over his chin, tasted flat and luke-warm in his mouth. Agony stabbed through his chest. He struggled, smashing at the yielding water with his hands, fighting back to higher ground. He stood breast deep, scowling at the water that had attacked him. He had no fear, simply dislike, and a conviction that he had been treated unfairly. He wanted to go to the hills, and the river was trying to stop him. But he would not let it. If pain there must be; so be it. He stepped forward.

This time he ignored the agony in his chest and walked on, straight through the watery darkness that engulfed him. And finally, as if realizing its defeat, the pain went away. The water kept pushing at him, pulling his feet off the soft muddy bottom, but each time his head broke the water he could see that he was making progress.

The twisting chest pain came back as he emerged at last into shallower water. Water sprayed from his lips. He coughed and retched until tears blurred his vision, and for a while he lay contorted on the grassy bank. The paroxysm ended. He climbed to his feet, and for a long minute stood staring at the dark, rushing stream. When he turned away, he was conscious of one thing: He didn't like water.

The road puzzled him when he came to it. It stretched in an almost straight line toward the western horizon; and its very uniformity gave it character. It was obvious that, like himself, it had a purpose, but it wasn't actively going anywhere. He tried to think of it as a river that was not moving, but he felt no sense of repulsion, no dislike; and when he stepped on it he didn't sink into it.

A sound drew him out of his mental effort. It came from the north where the road wound into sight from behind a tree-covered hill. At first he saw nothing, then the thing came into sight. Part of the thing's body was like his own. That part had arms, legs, body and head, almost exactly as he had. Its face was white, but the rest was mostly dark in color. And there all resemblance to himself ended. Below the curious image of himself was a wooden thing with wheels; and in front of that a sleek, scarlet, four-legged thing with one horn sticking out of the center of its head.

Ptath moved straight toward the beast, eyes wide, mind grasping at details. He heard the top part of the thing yell at him, and then the nose with the horn on it caught him in the chest. The animal stopped.

Ptath picked himself off the gravel angrily. The man part of the creature was still yelling at him; and it wasn't that he didn't understand. It was simply that the thing was standing up, shaking its arms at him. *It wasn't attached.* Like himself, it was separate, different. He heard it say:

"What's the matter with you, walking right into my dottle? Are you sick? And what's the idea of wandering around naked? Do you want the soldiers of the goddess to see you?"

There was too much meaning, too many words piling one on top of another. His anger faded before his effort to bring all the words together into one whole.

"Matter?" he repeated finally. "Sick?"

The man stared at him curiously. "Say," the fellow said slowly, "you are sick. You'd better climb up here beside me and I'll take you to the temple at Linn. It's only five kanbs away; and they'll feed you and give you medical attention there. Here, I'll come down and give you a hand up."

As the dottle started forward the man said: "What happened to your clothes?"

"Clothes?" Ptath said curiously.

"Sure." The man stared at him. "By the zard of Accadistran, you mean to say you don't know you're naked? Looks like amnesia to me."

Ptath shifted uneasily. There was a quality in the fellow's tone that he didn't like, a suggestion that something was wrong with him. He glared the beginning of anger and said loudly:

"Naked! Clothes!"

"Don't get excited." The man sounded startled. He said hastily, "Look—clothes, like this!"

He fumbled at his own rough coat, held up an edge of it. Rage evaporated out of Ptath. He stared at the man, trying to comprehend that the fellow was not really dark in color, but that a dark something *covered* him. He snatched at the coat and drew it closer the better to examine it. There was a tearing sound, and a piece of cloth came free in his fingers.

The man let out a yell, "Hey, what in—"

Ptath turned a puzzled gaze on the fellow. The thought in his mind was that this creature who made so much noise wanted him to stop looking at the coat. Abruptly impatient, he shoved the torn section back. But it didn't seem to be enough. The man's eyes were narrowed, his lips twisted, as he said:

"You ripped that cloth as if it was so much paper. You're not sick. You're—"

Decision hardened his face. His hands jerked up, shoved furiously. There was no resisting an action that had no meaning until it was over. Ptath struck the ground with a jar. He was too angry to be aware of pain. With a grunt he jumped to his feet and saw that the cart was moving rapidly along the road to the west. The one-horned dottle was running in great, galloping strides. And the man was standing erect in the cart, lashing at the animal with the reins.

Ptath trudged along the road thinking of the dottle and cart. It would be pleasant to ride in the cart all the way to Ptath.

It was a long time after that the great beasts appeared on the road far ahead. He watched them and felt his first tightening interest as he saw that men were on their backs. The trick, of course, was to get up close to the rider and shove him off fast. And ride rapidly away down the road. He waited, trembling in his eagerness. Puzzlement came only when the four animals came near.

They were bigger than he had thought. They towered. They were twice as tall as he was, and massively built. Their necks were long and supported small, wicked-looking, three-horned heads. The bright yellow of their necks contrasted vividly with their green bodies and the bluish violet of their long, tapering tails. They pounded up quickly and reared to a halt in a cloud of dust.

"That's him all right," said one of the men. "The farmer described him exactly."

"Fine-looking chap," a second said. "Just how are we going to handle him?"

A third frowned. "I've seen him somewhere. I'm sure of it. Can't just place him, though."

They had come for him because somebody had described him to them. The man with the dottle, of course, his enemy. The why of it was beyond his comprehension, but it only stiffened his determination. The long, sloping tail, he thought carefully, offered the best method of climbing, but that way the rider would know his purpose. Actually the best approach would be a variation of the one the man had used on him.

He said, "Will you help me up? It is five kanbs to Linn, and they will feed me and give me medical attention at the temple there. Come down and give me a handup. I am sick and have no clothes."

It sounded convincing in his own ears. He waited, watching their reaction, alert to every word and gesture, noting phrases for future study, grim with his purpose. The men looked at each other, then they laughed. Finally, one said tolerantly:

"Sure, fellow, we'll give you a lift. That's what we're here for."

Another said, "You've got your distances slightly mixed, stranger. Linn is three kanbs away, not five." He laughed. "You're lucky you turned out to be harmless. We thought it was some rebel stunt. Throw him the clothes we brought along, Dallird."

A bundle landed in the grass beside the road. Ptath fumbled at it curiously, laid each piece out on the green, studying from the corners of his eyes the way the men were dressed. There were a few extras in the bundle which he examined and finally tossed aside as unnecessary. He saw that the men were watching him with wide grins.

"You stupid idiot," one said abruptly, "don't you know anything about clothes! Look, that's underclothing. It goes on underneath. You put it on first."

Ptath's mind was quicker now. There were more facts on which to build. In a flash of understanding he grasped at the words and in two minutes he was dressed. He walked up to one of the animals and held up his hand to the man, Dallird, who had thrown him the clothes.

"Up," he said. "Help me up."

The version of his plan that had suddenly occurred to him was as simple as it was effective. The man reached down, said:

"Take my hand and grab hold of the saddle."

That was easy. It was all easy. Ptath pulled himself up with one effortless contraction of the muscles of one arm. With the other he jerked at the man's hand. Dallird yelped shrilly as he soared out of his saddle. He landed on his knees and was crouching there, groaning and cursing as Ptath pulled himself firmly into the saddle, caught up the reins, wheeled the animal toward the west and beat at it with the reins as it ran just as he had seen the man do with the dottle.

The swift ride fascinated him. There was no jar, no up-and-down movement, no swaying. The dottle cart had been bumpy; this was a flow, a dreamlike rhythm. There was no doubt about it, he would travel all the rest of his journey this way.

He was watching the galloping motion of the beast's hind legs, and the way the seemingly heavy tail floated in the air behind the great animal, when his glance caught a part of the road behind him. There, a few lengths away, were the other three beasts, one with two men mounted on it.

They made an interesting, colorful picture, strung out at full racing gallop. It was absorbing to watch them so near him, drawing closer, closer. He felt no dismay, no sense of being personally involved. What finally brought a thin frown to his face was the way the mouths of the men opened and shut. The sound of their shouting penetrated to him above the pounding of the paws of his own beast. Their yells startled him. They were after him, and it wasn't right. He had not chased the man on the cart. It was becoming clear that he had made a mistake.

With a gathering dislike he watched the beasts draw abreast of him. Whipping his own animal did no good. It was slower than the others, or else these men knew some mysterious way of getting speed out of their mounts. Two of the big beasts were pushing with their long necks against the head of his mount. It slowed, then began to rear, then stopped.

Ptath sat angry and nonplused. The situation was absolutely new, different, and strange. Unless he could think of some drastic action, these men might try to force him off the back of the animal.

One of the men spoke: "Well, we've got him cornered. Now what?"

"Let me get a poke at him," snarled Dallird. "I'll punch that handsome face of his to a bloody pulp."

Ptath glared at the man. He wasn't sure what the words meant, but there was a suggestion of further shoving, and his neck muscles swelled in answering rage. A vague plan that had been in the back of his mind leaped to the fore. It seemed abruptly a simple and satisfactory solution.

He would knock all the men off their mounts, drive the beasts in front of him for a distance, and thus with one action prevent the men from following him and from sending out others to annoy him.

He saw that one of the men was drawing a long, pointed thing from a scabbard that lay across the back of the man's own mount. The pointed thing flashed up high into the air.

"Get off!" the man cried. "Get down to the road or I'll hit you over the head with my spear."

"Why not stick it into him?" urged Dallird. "Teach him not to interfere with temple soldiers."

Ptath's mind blazed with anger, with a sense of outrage, and a fierce determination to carry out his purpose. There was a way, he saw, that it might be worked against Dallird and the man mounted with him. The beast they rode was just beyond easy arm's reach. By hanging onto the saddle with his fingers, slipping his left leg over and reaching swiftly—

That would leave him open to the attack from the man with the spear and the man on the third beast; but it was already clear that he would have to carry out his plan by stages. With a sliding movement he snatched at the two men. A fist landed on his face. It stung, but it was the novelty of it, not the pain that made him retaliate in kind. His knuckles crashed into the face of the man beside Dallird. Bones cracked, blood spurted. The man crumpled back with a single cry and hung limply down from the saddle. It was such an effective method that

Ptath lashed at Dallird. The man shrank back, and half fell, half slid to the ground. He stood there shouting shrilly:

"Stick him, Bir, stick him! He's killed San."

Ptath jerked back into the saddle. He expected pain in his back, but nothing happened. The man with the spear was well down the road, disappearing over the crest of a hill. Ptath frowned and urged his own mount forward. His intention was to try to catch the fellow. But as he came to the rim of the great valley down which the road wound, he saw that the man was steadily widening the gap between them. He disappeared into a distant grove of trees.

The road kept twisting gently to the right as Ptath plunged down into the valley. It curved past men working in the dark, grassless field, past curious-looking wooden and stone mounds that stood well back among the trees. It came finally to the clump of trees where Bir had disappeared, and divided neatly in two.

Astounded, Ptath pulled his beast to a halt. The spectacle of what he had come to accept as a perfectly normal road splitting into two roads of equal size was a major development that required long seconds to absorb. His tenseness yielded to the drab fact. The roads just lay there. One section continued rightward; the other turned westward onto a great plain, westward toward distant Ptath. He had been on the west road a long time when the sound came from the sky.

The flying beast swept low over him, its great blue-gray wings flapping explosively, its long, triangular head poking down, peering at him from livid, fire-colored eyes. It was not until it swung back toward him that he saw that one of the two men mounted on its back was the man, Bir. Ptath stiffened. The man had gone to get this enormous flying thing so that he could continue to annoy him. This persistent pursuit was becoming unbearable. Ptath shook his fist at the bird and shouted, the way the riders of the long-necked beasts had done to him. The flying beast circled him once more, then whirled off ahead, flying swiftly. It became a spot in the sky, vanished in the blue mists of the west.

Ptath rode on. Suddenly, the sun, which he had scarcely noticed when it was high above him, appeared well down toward the western horizon, directly over a gathering cloud of dust. The dust came nearer, dissolved finally into a long line of beasts like his own, each with a rider. Above the racing animals soared a host of bluish-gray flying things.

The great concourse swept toward him; a solid wave of a score of animals engulfed him. Something long and thin, like an elongated rein, flicked at him. Instantly, his arms were pinioned, and he was jerked to the ground. He landed on his hands and knees; and for a moment the confusion was complete. Beasts milled around him. There were shouts, a bedlam that made thinking hard. At last, almost blankly, he climbed to his feet. He snatched at the lasso, and with one jerk flung it aside. Free of that restraint, he grew conscious that he was dismounted once more, and that the whole process of obtaining an animal to ride must be gone through again.

His eyes narrowed; his gaze flashed to the faces of the riders surrounding him, searching for Bir. He wasn't there; and that was good. That meant they wouldn't know about his version of the trick. He thought for a moment, considering intently the exact words he should use in view of what he had heard and seen. Then he said:

"Someone come down and give me a hand up. It is only three kanbs to Linn and they will feed me at the temple there and give me medical attention. I—"

He stopped at that point because his gaze fell on a—not man. The creature resembled the others, but in place of shorts she wore a long dark gown; and instead of sitting in a saddle on the neck of the mount, she rode in a box under a canopy that was strapped to the broad back of the gigantic animal. The woman spoke in a rich contralto:

"My lord," she said, "that is the strangest speech I have ever heard. Is the man mad?"

A tall man with iron-gray hair said, "I'm afraid so. I forgot to tell you, daughter, that the screer rider, knowing we were homeward bound, flew out to warn us that we would meet this fellow. It seems he has already committed murder. Captain, inform the temple princess of the situation."

Ptath listened to the explanation with interest. There were puzzling things about it, words that conjured up no pictures, but enough came clear to bring quick anger at the distorted account. But it did not occur to him to correct the story, or even that anything more would grow out of the affair.

The simple fact was that, starting with the man in the dottle cart, there had been a whole series of attempts to prevent him from riding. It was very irritating, but their numbers were now so great that, for the time being at least he had better accept the situation. He would continue on foot. The decision made, he turned, stooped under the great green belly of a beast, and started off along the road.

A soft cool breeze was blowing. It brushed steadily against his cheeks as he walked. It brought with it a strong but not unpleasant odor of sweating animals; and a thin perfume of grass, trees and plowed fields and grain that stood low and green; the whole combining into a rich, heady mixture that was exhilarating. Discord came abruptly as a shout rent the air. There was a stirring of animals, and a great milling and stamping. Then they had him surrounded again. The woman said softly:

"Even for a madman, his psychology is strange. What are you going to do with him, my lord?"

The man shrugged. "Execute him, of course. Murder is murder." He nodded to the captain: "Dismount six men. Take him into that plowed field and bury him. A three-foot grave will do."

Ptath watched curiously as the men dismounted. The words the man called 'my lord' had spoken had meaning of a sort, but there was so much new in them that his mind would build no pictures. And the very quiet seriousness of the tone added dimness and abstractness to a situation that was becoming more puzzling by the second.

Reality came sharply as two men he had not noticed stepped from behind him and grabbed his elbows. The action was so personal that he shoved them violently away. The men went flying into the dirt. Ptath turned irritably as a third man dived for his knees. He staggered as the man's shoulder struck him, and he hit out fiercely at the fellow's head. The man slumped to the ground and lay there.

Ptath stepped clear of the fallen body, and was grabbed around the body and arms by two of the remaining three; the third caught his legs. The trio lifted him clear of the ground, and that was unendurable. With a single kick he smashed at the face of the man who held his legs. Instantly, back on his feet, Ptath snatched at the two other men, caught them, held them up for a moment, one twisting, struggling body in each hand, then flung them angrily aside.

He looked up then from the man 'my lord', to the woman, then back to the man. For the first time he blamed him for this inexplicable assault. His eyes blazed at the fellow and in a single glance measured the distance between himself and the other. If he could silence him as he had the others, this stupidity might end. He grew aware that the woman was speaking:

"I seem to have seen him before somewhere. Stranger, what is your name?"

The question stopped him at the beginning of his run. His name? Why, Ptath, of course. Ptath of Gonwonlane. Thrice greatest Ptath. He felt astounded that the question should have been asked at all. He shook his head, impatient of the shouts that made it almost impossible for his answer to reach the woman. My lord was yelling something about arrows; and, simultaneously, there was a poignant pain in Ptath's chest.

He looked down and was amazed to see a thin piece of wood protruding from his left breast. He stared at it blankly for a moment, then pulled it out and threw it on the ground. The pain vanished. A second arrow pinned his arm to his body. He tore that out too; and once more he turned to the man who was causing him all this trouble. He heard the woman cry out:

"My lord, stop them, stop them! Didn't you hear what he said? Don't you see?"

"Eh?" The man turned toward her. Ptath, struggling in a rising fury with a third arrow, heard the puzzled note in his voice.

"Don't you see?" the woman answered. *"He whose strength is unlimited, who tires not, and knows no fear—"*

The man's voice lashed out: "What madness are you talking? That's a myth we keep alive for the masses. We've agreed a thousand times that the Goddess Ineznia uses the name, Ptath, as propaganda." He broke off: "Why, it's impossible."

She screamed, "Stop them! He's come back after ages of being merged with the race. Look closely! His face! Like the statue in the temple."

"Or like Prince Ineznio, the goddess' lover," said the man. "But never mind. Let me handle this."

The hysteria faded from the woman's face; her eyes narrowed. "Not here," she said quickly. "Get him to the temple."

My lord spoke to his men, then said quietly to Ptath: "You will come with us to the temple at Linn. We will feed you and give you medical attention, and then we will give you a flying screer that will take you where you want to go."

As swiftly as that the incomprehensible attack ended.

CHAPTER II

A Goddess In Chains

IN THE DEPTHS OF THE GREAT CITADEL PALACE OF THE CITY OF Ptath the dark, glorious woman sighed drearily. The stone floor where she lay huddled was damp and cold. In all the ages of her imprisonment she had never yet succeeded in warming the chill out of the enlacing metal chains that sagged endlessly on top of her. From where she lay she could see the chair where the golden-haired woman sat laughing with triumph, could hear that soft, ringing laughter which ended as the golden woman said in a rich, clear voice:

"And do you doubt me now, L'onee darling? Once again it is the old story. Do you remember the time when you refused to believe that I could imprison you? Yet here you are.

"And do you remember when I first came down here to tell you that I intended to destroy mighty Ptath, how you reminded me that only the two of us could bring him back; that I would have to use you as a pole of power, and that that would require your consent? Yet here he is. And you know now that I used you as a pole of power *without* your consent. Perhaps at last you are beginning to realize that while you waited with trusting simplicity for your Ptath to live his myriad human spans, I learned the potent vastness of the godpower he had given into our care."

The dark woman stirred. Her cold lips parted. She said in a weary yet steely, contemptuous voice:

"You traitor, Ineznia!"

In the half light, a smile played around the lips of the other woman. "How naive we are," she said softly. "And yet how clearly your every word shows that you realize I cannot fail to win. Those biting words of yours will seem very empty indeed when Ptath is dead, and you are dead, forever."

The dark woman sat up. Something of the intensity of her

spirit showed in the fire that was suddenly in her voice. "We're not dead yet, either of us. And now that you have watched him in action do you not feel just a little bit alarmed, Ineznia? The dynamic reality of Ptath, even though you have him in Gonwonlane before his time, even though he arrived stripped of power, the sheer violence of his personality must"—a sardonic note crept into her voice—"must surely have caused you a tiny doubt.

"And don't forget, darling Ineznia, don't forget the spells he set up in the long ago to protect himself from just such a danger as you now threaten. Seven spells, Ineznia, no more, no less. But the pattern is that only he can render them harmless."

She finished mockingly, "I can picture you trying to persuade the untamed ego of an elemental and immensely wilful Ptath to do what you desire. A Ptath, moreover, who is moment by moment becoming more cunning, and hourly growing in mental stature. Time flies, Ineznia, precious, irreplaceable time."

For a moment, as she finished, the small stone dungeon rang with her satiric laughter. The sound died. Abruptly conscious that she was wasting her strength, L'onee sank back to her prostrate position.

And saw that she had made no impression.

There was an expression of pleasure on the lovely child-face of the Goddess Ineznia, the joy of an animal that has succeeded in rousing the futile rebellion of an utterly helpless victim.

"How strange," Ineznia purred, "that you have thought of the very things for which I have all the answers. I would indeed be playing with fire if I permitted Ptath to develop and learn in a normal fashion—*as Ptath*. Perhaps you have forgotten that he has had many human personalities. The last of these I shall bring to the fore; to dominate, to confuse and to be confused.

"As for those lovely little spells, how easily they will be destroyed! The main one, as you know, is the god-chair in the palace of the Nushir of Nushirvan. To reach it, Ptath will have to conquer Nushirvan. I shall leave that to the ingenuity of his human personality, and to the great armies I shall furnish him. Actually, I have several alternative plans. So long as that chair exists, I can never command all the power of Gonwonlane. It is the potent symbol of his supremacy.

"I must persuade him, or force him, to cross the river of boiling mud, which has all these years prevented me from reaching the chair. I need hardly say that I will require only a few hours to destroy the chair, once I get to it.

"The other spells I shall weave into the pattern of the greater one. He must make love to me, as a recognition of my godhood. He must experience the power flow of a prayer stick, sign your death warrant, come with me in a journey of minds, go consciously through the realm of darkness, and, as I have said, cross the river of boiling mud.

"But now, L'onee darling, I must leave you. The procession escorting Ptath is approaching the temple of Linn; and I must take possession of the mind of the temple princess, and *be there*, on the scene, controlling, shaping events—"

As the dark woman watched, Ineznia sank deeper into her chair and closed her eyes. The pressure of her strong presence faded; slowly, the dungeon grew dim. The two bodies, the silent, enchained form of L'onee, the deathly still, seated shape of Ineznia, seemed shadows projected from some greater darkness.

The days passed.

CHAPTER III

The Man From 1944 A.D.

THE TEMPLE WAS A REGION OF DARK, LOWERING SKIES AND enclosing horizons. Uneasily conscious of those near walls and the ceiling pressing down at him, Ptath stared at the food on the table.

Mists rose from it, and an exudation of heat and above all, a tantalizing odor that pleasantly tickled his nostrils. From the narrow end of the table, my lord's voice suggested that he sit down. Puzzled, Ptath did so.

He had missed nothing during his ride to the temple of Linn. His senses, whetted by hard experience, quickened by new thoughts, had registered everything. The circular town, the temple itself that rose white and tall from the small forest of trees, around which the other buildings clustered. That temple which had so curiously lost its whiteness as he entered.

He saw that the others were sitting. There was my lord and the temple princess, dark and intense, her hair lustrous in the gloom, her eyes shining like the water that had given him pain. The difference was that he had no sense of unpleasantness. The several men in dark robes he scarcely noticed. They were nameless creatures who had slipped almost noiselessly into the room. They sat with expressionless faces, watching him from eyes that were uniformly black.

"All is well"—it was the woman; her voice a hissing sound in the stillness—"he has never seen food before."

Ptath looked at her quickly. There was something about the way she said it that he didn't like. She smiled a swift little smile that made her look so dazzling he forgot his irritation.

My lord said, "Careful! Let us eat, and see if he follows suit."

"I am sure," said the woman after a little, "that it is quite unnecessary to guard our tongues. He has come back mindless. He knows nothing. *Look* at him.''

It was the first taste that did it. Ptath gulped on without thought, or further attention to the others. The food was warm and good. Each bite thrilled his tongue. He did not even notice the instruments beside the plate. Oddly, the bites grew progressively distasteful. He pushed the plate away finally, scowling at it.

"Where is the screer?" he said matter-of-factly. "I will now fly to Ptath."

It was the woman who stood up, smiling. "This way," she said.

My lord half rose as she passed his chair, put a restraining hand on her arm. "Are you sure—" he began anxiously.

"We can only lose our lives," the woman answered. "If we win, our reward may be a temple kingdom, a city empire. Father, I assure you I know what I am doing."

The princess smiled at Ptath, who had followed the conversation with a dim comprehension. "This way!" she said; and her voice was so strong and confident that once more his vague doubts faded. "The screer is waiting down these steps."

Her smile drew him. He liked her for a reason that wasn't clear. He followed her. He could almost feel himself flying through the air, the way the man, Bir, had flown above him, and the other screers on the journey to Linn. The mental picture was exhilarating.

The steps led farther down than he remembered coming up. But finally the downward part ended. There was a level of hard floor. Glowing sticks stood at intervals along the broad corridor, and there were many closed doors. The woman paused before a door that stood open.

"Through there," she smiled. She motioned with her arm and touched his hand with a curious gliding movement of her palm. Her flesh felt soft and warm. It made his whole being tingle with liking for her.

Ptath stepped across the threshold, and found himself in a tiny room with a very low sky. A single light stick hung from the ceiling of the otherwise bare room. *Thud!* The sound came from behind him. Ptath turned and saw that the door had closed. He stood there blankly as a small stone slot clinked open. The woman's face appeared in it.

"Do not be alarmed, Ptath," she said. "We have changed our minds about giving you a screer. We are sending to Ptath for your wife, the glorious Ineznia. She will come and take you back to the great city. This is your room until she arrives."

"By Accadistran!" My lord's voice exclaimed in the corridor. "You don't really expect him to remain so quiet—"

The slot snapped shut. The voice cut off as if it had been broken. Abruptly, the light blinked out. There was silence. And darkness.

Ptath stood uncertain in the blackness. He kept expecting the door to open with the announcement that glorious Ineznia—that was the name the temple princess had used; he remembered every syllable of its pronunciation—had arrived to take him to Ptath.

Time passed. Impatience grew in him, the conviction that he could have reached Ptath by now even if he had had to walk. Thought of walking brought the comparison idea of sitting. The floor was cold and hard, but he sat there and waited. And waited and waited. And waited.

Miasmas drifted like so much smoke through his mind. Thought forms came that had no meaning, strange half thoughts, and one idea of incredible lucidity: This was mad, it said. Something was wrong. He must do something. It took a long, long time to decide what. But finally he climbed to his feet, a titanic rage flaring in his mind. He tried the door, lunging at it with all his terrible strength. But it held. It did not even shudder from the plunging weight of his body.

Curiously, then, he was sitting again on the floor—curiously, because he had no conscious memory of having seated himself. Time passed. The darkness and the silence became separate, palpable forces that distorted the even flow of life currents in his body, unsteadied the positive continuity of his will, and brought changes—incredible thoughts.

"Keep the tank going. Nurse that engine . . . We're almost over . . . over—Watch out . . . There's a dive bomber . . . Watch . . . He got us—"

Blackout.

For uncounted ages, Holroyd's body strained against darkness. In that darkness was no past, no present, no future, simply a cold hardness of damp stone that bruised his bones and pressed with blind, deadly force against his flesh. Slowly but surely that unrelenting coldness was drawing the warm life out of him.

Holroyd came to consciousness with a start. He had the impression of emerging from a restless, nightmarish sleep, but no sleep ever had such an awakening. His fingers fumbled over a chill stone floor he couldn't see because of the intensity of the blackness of that room.

He tried to sit up; and, because it did not occur to him that he couldn't, because his mind did not even remotely accept this blackness as real, this damp stone as his bed—he reached a sitting posture before the first sick surge of dizziness stabbed at his reason. He sat there blank-brained, his body racked by the frightful nausea. The enveloping night whirled insensately, and the cold of the floor was like a wind that sucked at his bones. And then—from somewhere inside him rage came. A blazing fury of mortal rage, somehow *directed*, somehow based on understanding of why he was here.

"Damn her!" he railed. "Oh, damn the temple princess!"

An unnatural quality in the meaning of that booming blast of echoing sound startled him. Anger drained from him; and after a long moment a childlike wonder struck into his consciousness.

"Temple princess!" he repeated aloud, and cocked his head, straining to penetrate the alien core of that phrase. But for a long, dead-blank time his painful concentration yielded nothing. Slowly, his brain grasped again at its dim train of idea.

"Temple princess!" he said once more. But this time there was no voice in him; and the words were little more than a hoarse ripple in the black stillness. It was sheer amazement that brought a flow of strength. He exclaimed aloud:

"Why, there's nothing like that in America. Or in the part of Germany where we're fighting. Maybe North Africa—No!"

There was madness here, a fantastic madness that pounded at his temples as he half lowered himself, half fell back, dazed from the effort of his brief thoughts and briefer movements. For a time he sprawled there, his mind on the very verge of an abyss of night. Vague, measured thought forms floated sluggishly into it, a gentle stirring of a vast, devastating complexity of memory that included the equally slow, equally tremendous realization that his words, except for the place names, had been spoken in a language at once foreign and familiar, a language so sweet in the soft harmony of its speech that the very words—America, Germany, North Africa—had been like discordant hammer blows interrupting a concert, harsh, cacophonous and barbarous.

"Say, you who call yourself Ptath!" It was a man's voice, deep and melodious, out of the near darkness.

That was for him. Holroyd struggled to turn over. But the cold had him now, as if he were encased in ice. He gave up and lay still, but his mind fastened, leechlike, on the name word. His lips moved, his voice muttered:

"Holroyd Ptath! No, that's not right. Must be Ptath Holroyd. No, Holroyd is an American. Peter Holroyd, captain, 290th tank brigade, and—But who is Ptath?"

The question was like a key to a tightly locked door. Memory came. He said aloud, in explosive amazement: "I'm—mad!"

Ptath, the god of Gonwonlane, whose last human personality, that of Peter Holroyd, tank-corps captain, had emerged from the hidden deeps of his brain under mind-destroying stress, sat up.

"Damn it!" he said. "I'm Holroyd. That other stuff is—"

Holroyd stopped, shuddering with a dim horror, a quaver of fear, a sharp consciousness of the intensity of that other almost mindless self.

"This is crazy!" he thought wildly. "Crazy!"

But after a minute it was all still there: the dark room, the other mind, the knowledge that he was alive, who had been in a tank squarely hit by a German bomb. And there was abrupt awareness of something else, remembrance of the voice that had spoken to him, the voice that had called him—Ptath.

No, that was wrong. The voice hadn't called him Ptath. The voice had said: "You who call yourself Ptath!" There was a subtle difference in the meaning that made Holroyd frown with thought. He lay very still, thinking of the things that Ptath had seen on the road and in the temple. His whole being began to tremble with a nameless wonder. Horror pulsed against his mind. It was the passing seconds that brought surcease, and awareness of the double identity that was inside him.

Whatever it was couldn't hurt him physically. It was a part of him. Or, rather, he was a part of it, but for some reason he dominated, his thought, his personality, his—self. He began to feel better. The tenseness went out of his muscles. His whole being relaxed.

The rasp of heavy breathing broke the silence of the darkness that engulfed him. Then came an undertone of cursing: "Where in Nushirvan is that light. It should be in this corner—Ah!"

A pale white light flickered on, revealing what Holroyd had already recollected; a small, bare concrete room with a solid stone floor. Not exactly solid. A slab of stone in the corner beside the door had been neatly pushed up and laid aside. Where it had been, barely visible from Holroyd's prostrate position, was the entrance to a tunnel.

Slowly, painfully, Holroyd twisted his head toward the source of the light. A small man was standing directly under the glowing stick, staring at him. The fellow was neatly dressed in shorts and a tucked-in shirt. He had shining eyes in a round, cheerful face that creased slowly into a frown as he stared at Holroyd.

"Say," he said, "you look in a bad way. I should have come before, I guess, but I didn't know which cell they'd put you in, and besides, I've been waiting for them to come to feed you." He screwed his lips up thoughtfully. "Funny, they haven't done that. But never mind. I've got some soup down in the tunnel that ought to go pretty good." He bounded across to the hole. "I'll have it up for you in a spasm."

The soup was warm and life-giving. It tingled deliciously in his mouth and trickled like dull fire down into his body. It soothed; it eased the dreadful chill of his flesh, and brought a sense of approaching well-being. As he sipped, Holroyd listened to the babble of words the little man poured at him.

"Name's Tar, representing all the prisoners in the Linn temple, and welcoming you to our ranks. Naturally, our organization here is associated with the rebels, and betrayal of us means death. That's all you need to know.

"We know all that's known about you, of course," the man chattered on. "You claim to be Ptath. That's a good line. That's new. Nobody ever thought of it before. Maybe the rebels can use you if you are prepared to carry that pretense on. But more than that, the farmer who picked you up on the road says you've got amnesia.''

The effort necessary to keep himself from swallowing the soup at one gulp made it hard to concentrate. For long his mind seemed incapable of anything but listening. But abruptly Holroyd grew aware of a strange and terrible thing. Something inside him—something—was listening with his mind to every word that Tar was uttering. Listening intently, with a steely consciousness of the meaning of what was being said. It was a long, blank moment before he realised that the something was—himself.

Holroyd could feel the chill of the concrete against which he leaned. Warming his fingers was the long, narrow tumbler of clear soup. And all around, so closely around, was the damp and formidable dungeon cell. The awareness of his environment was more acute than at any time since his first consciousness of it; and yet it was overshadowed by the grim fact of that other, greater being who in some curious and unpleasant way had become intimately integrated with his own personality. The two were one, yet there were two. Holroyd groaned inwardly: So that was what amnesia was like—when you remembered the other self. He sat intent on the problem involved, shaken by the identity that other self had claimed, and by his memory of the things that it had done.

The temple princess had said she was sending for someone called the Goddess Ineznia. Until this instant the name had been in the background of his mind, a normal memory. But now his brain paused. Sending for *whom?*

The soup was all gone. He clung to the tumbler because of its warmth. It was the only warmth there was. His brain was a frozen thing inside his head. The Goddess Ineznia! The title roared in his mind. He swayed, and curious little darknesses slithered through his mind. A thought shaped finally, a thought so sharp that it seemed to pierce his being like a hard-driven knife. He had to get out of here. No matter who Ptath was, Peter Holroyd couldn't handle a situation like this. He had to get out—unless it was already too late.

His eyes widened with the possibility. He felt a feverish

fear. Every muscle tensed, he glared at the little man. "How long"—his voice was a croaking sound in his own ears—"have I been here?"

The moment he had spoken he realised that he had interrupted the other, and that Tar had been chattering steadily from the first moment. The man broke off, frowning:

"That's what I've been telling you. The stories about you say that you were as strong as a grimb; and yet, seven days without food and water, I find you like this. Practically dead—"

The man said more, but Holroyd didn't hear. Seven days, he mused. For seven days the god Ptath had lain here slowly going mad, and finally the stress had become so great that he had lapsed to his last reincarnation. The thought jangled because—so much deterioration in seven days? Impossible.

The time involved was more like seven years or even seven hundred years. Ptath, who had no conception of time, lying in a timeless darkness may have experienced time *faster than his surroundings*. That was the only possible explanation of such a tremendous final result. Once again Holroyd's thought ended with violence. He sat blankly amazed at himself, at the very idea that he could even have such a conception. What kind of madness was this that afflicted him? Seven hundred years in seven days! He licked dry lips, clenched his mind and concentrated on seven days.

"How long," he said aloud, "would it take a"—his twentieth-century brain paused before the word, then with an effort he spoke it—"a flying screer to fly from here to Ptath and back?"

The bright eyes of Tar were regarding him oddly. "You're a funny fellow," he said finally. "There was some story about your being on your way to Ptath. But that only proves you must have been in a bad way before they put you in here."

He shook his head, and Holroyd had the sudden feeling that he was being deliberately frustrated. His impulse was to snatch at the man and tear the answer out of him. His mind rocked with savage anger. At the last instant he recognized the unnatural fury as not of Holroyd. He caught himself, and said shakily:

"But how long . . . how long would it take?"

"You don't understand," the man replied. "Your question is silly. No screer has ever been flown from Linn direct to Ptath. It's too far. The time the temple princess made the trip, she flew north to the sea city of Tamardee, then on to Lapisar and gorgeous Ghay, and so on along the coast. Altogether the trip took two months.

"Mind you," Tar went on, "there are supposed to be really fast breeds of birds. They say that some of the goddess' messengers' riding especially trained thoroughbreds can fly from one end of Gonwonlane to the other in a little over eight days without stopovers. That would be six days from here to Ptath. But now, listen—"

Holroyd sighed. Six days there and six days back. The goddess knew, had known for a full day now. Five more days and she would be here.

He had just five days to escape from the temple dungeon.

CHAPTER IV

200,000,000 Years In The Future

THE SHORTNESS OF THE TIME INVOLVED WAS NOT REALLY depressing at first. Holroyd felt no urge to get up, or even to think, while he waited for Tar to bring more soup. He did wonder about the source of the soup, and of the other food that Tar, before he scuttled back into his hole, had promised for later meals. The awareness that came finally, however, was startling.

A part of him did not worry. It *waited* for the arrival of the goddess. Cold and intent it waited, an untamed force unconscious of limitations, accepting the knowledge of Holroyd's brain in the same fashion it had earlier accepted its own identity, its own purpose.

The feeling was strong and utterly unmistakable. Sitting there, Holroyd had no doubt at all. Ptath, the child-like god of Gonwonlane and Peter Holroyd were inhabiting the same body and the god considered Holroyd as one segment of his being. Which he was. Holroyd shuddered, and then experienced a wild, personal rage.

"You idiot!" he shouted. "Don't you realise what a mess you've got us into, letting a pretty, smiling face lure you into this dungeon? The veriest sap would need to take only one look at the tyranny set-up of temple prince, temple king, temple emperor, with the goddess somewhere at the top of that hierarchy to know that your arrival was pure dynamite. You can't—"

He stopped. His voice reverberated briefly in the narrow confines of the cell. In the silence that followed, Holroyd thought with a wry weariness: What a hopeless outburst, a madman shouting advice to himself. But he felt better for it, more conscious suddenly that he was in charge of the body, his mind doing the thinking, controlling the vocal cords.

As for that basic god-confidence of Ptath, it wouldn't hurt to have it there. Wouldn't hurt during crises to know that there was a part of him that had no fear, no doubt of its own capabilities, but lived on with a savage certainty of its right to everything. It wouldn't hurt to *feel* unkillable.

The second time Tar came he brought more soup, and a big, green citrus fruit. It was amazingly juicy and sweet, the flavor delicious and unlike anything Holroyd had ever tasted. The taste of it, the concrete reality of its strangeness brought a question that had not come even in embryo from the earlier abstract thought and memory that had racked him. Where was Gonwonlane? Where was a land with cities called Ptath and Tamardee and Lapisar and Ghay? Gorgeous Ghay, Tar had said. Holroyd tried to picture that. And couldn't. It had no meaning; the vision of splendor evoked was only a misty version of some of the cities he had seen on 1944 Earth, alive with their slums, their bleak streets, their depressing commercial life. He intoned the names aloud: Gonwonlane, Ptath— there was a rhythm in them, a strange sweetness of sound that was like music.

The need to know grew stronger. Where was Gonwonlane? In a tingling excitement he turned to ask Tar and saw that he was alone. The stone was in place.

Holroyd was still lying there a timeless period later when the stone moved, and Tar came up. He had more fruit, and some bread, soft, white bread, newly baked. Holroyd seized the precious, familiar food and the tears blurred his vision. He felt amazement at the depth of the reaction, a brief shame. But the shame faded. It was good to know that wherever Gonwonlane might be, it was joined to the twentieth century by endless streams of bread. He had a picture of thousands of miles and years of bread stretching into the past and into the future, the staple diet of a vast portion of the people of Earth forever. He parted his lips but it was Tar who spoke.

"I've been wondering," the little man said matter-of-factly, "about that amnesia business. You're getting along like chain lightning physically, but what about your mind? If you could read that would be the quickest method of solving the problem."

"Read?" echoed Holroyd. And felt an immense astonishment. He had not once thought of books in Gonwonlane.

"Sure—look!" Tar jerked a folder from a pocket inside his shirt and held it out. Holroyd took the silky-smooth yet stiff paper and stared at words that could have blared straight out of a communist manifesto:

THE IMPORTANCE OF
AN ATTACK ON
ACCADISTRAN

The foul action of the zard of Accadistran in using the outlaws of Nushirvan to kidnap Gonwonlanian citizens demands retributive war on the largest scale. The government of the goddess Ineznia must be forced to launch an attack on this scoundrel.

Our efforts must be concentrated on persuading more and more people to change their prayers, those prayers which in their totality create the godpower of the goddess. The people must—

"All right, you can read." The little man snatched the folder from Holroyd's fingers. "I can see by the way you move your lips. I'll have some books up here in a spasm."

He lowered himself into the hole, became a head and shoulders that ducked into the nether depth. He returned almost immediately, carrying two quite normal-looking books.

"I'll be up before breakfast to collect those, so read as much of them as you can before you go to sleep. It's true they haven't fed you so far, but we can't take any chances. Give me those fruit rinds."

A minute later Holroyd was examining with trembling fingers the first of the two volumes. At first he merely thumbed hastily. He felt such a blazing eagerness to see everything that he caught only tantalizing glimpses of pictures and page after page of print. It *was* print, clear black ink impressed onto a white background. The paper was of a stiff but not too glossy material, and the pages were bound with something that looked like glue.

The pictures were all colored photographs, or else drawing done with such minute attention to detail that the illusion of photography was instantaneous. And the illusion remained as he riffled the pages with only an occasional excited pause for a more careful examination.

The book was titled *"History of Gonwonlane from the Earliest Times."* With deliberate will, Holroyd turned finally to page one of the text and read:

> "In the beginning was the Shining One, Ptath, god of land, sea and space, on whom be all praise heaped, and countless prayers offered that he may return to his chosen from his millions of years of merging with the race, which noble sacrifice he made for the glory of his people and for the development of his spirit, O Diyan, O Kolla and divine Rad."

Holroyd blinked at the words, then reread them frowningly, noting the reference to millions of years. A slow smile came finally. The author was being just a little too soulful, the cynical twist in the "lip" service too apparent. The second paragraph confirmed the impression, for it began without further preamble:

> "Earth is a very old planet, long inhabited by human beings. The continents and seas have suffered many cataclysmic changes, not the least of these being the gradual dissolution of ancient Gondwanaland and the equally gradual re-solution of this mightiest of all land masses."

Holroyd read the volume from beginning to end without a pause, then picked up the second book with an automatic and stupendous interest.

The title said: *"History of the World in Maps with Explanatory Text."* The cartographs showed Earth from remotest times, but the skillful, detailed drawings of the continents of long ago had an unreal quality that he couldn't seem to concentrate on. In the end only modern Gonwonlane mattered. It was a long and wide stretch of land that ran more than halfway around the southern hemisphere, bulged tremendously toward the north, and terminated at a point well east of what more than a hundred million years before had been, according to the text, "ancient Asdralia."

Gonwonlane was eleven thousand kanbs long, five thousand kanbs at its widest, and it was bounded in the northwest by the mountainous thousand-kanb-wide isthmus of Nushirvan. In an almost blank mental operation, Holroyd estimated that a kanb was one and a quarter miles. Then, he returned to his studying with a gaze that seemed glued to the page.

The land to the north of the Nushirvan isthmus, where ancient greater Ameriga and the continent of ancient Breton had once been, was labeled Accadistran. Only a series of large lakes marked where once had been the Atlantic Ocean. The body of water between Accadistran and Gonwonlane was called the Sea of Teths. The population of Gonwonlane was fifty-four billion, of Accadistran nineteen billion and of the outlaw state of Nushirvan five billion. Geologically, Nushirvan was the most recent land body on the planet, having rocketed out of the sea only thirty million years before.

The temple town of Linn, Holroyd located at the extreme east of the great southern land mass. The city of Ptath was eighty-three hundred kanbs from Linn to the northwest as the screer flies. Mighty Ptath itself was situated on the bay of the Great Cliff of the Teths Sea about twelve hundred kanbs from the nearest outjut of Nushirvan.

The wonder of it grew and grew. Holroyd kept climbing to his feet, pacing the floor, book in hand in a thrall of fascination. He reread whole sections of the history with its account of a goddess-ruled empire so vast that his mind alternately quailed and soared from the picturing of it. But slowly a conviction formed, a steeling of his mind, a heady certainty that there wasn't a soldier from the 1944 blitz of Germany who would really be fazed by such a situation as this.

He was dead. Except for this resurrection in the body of a god, he would be lying in a moldering tank on a battlefield so long forgotten that the soil, the memory, the very idea of it seemed already a curious and impossible tale.

A sound disturbed the hard brightness of his thought. The stone was moving. With a swift twisting movement, Holroyd strode over, bent, pulled the slab up with an effortless strength. His mind was cool and steady. He had a plan as simple as it was direct.

Tar's head popped up through the square opening. "Thanks," he puffed. "This moving of stones is wearing me down. I've got your breakfast."

"You've got my what?" Holroyd exclaimed. His singleness of purpose, his will to concentrate only on his plan, suffered an eclipse. He hadn't slept! He'd read all night without even thought of sleep. He sighed deeply. The reason was obvious, of course. Gods didn't sleep. Or at least they didn't need to. Perhaps he could if he tried. He saw that Tar was looking at him with surprised eyes.

"What's the matter?" Tar asked.

Holroyd shook his head. "Nothing. I didn't realize I'd slept so long."

The little man grinned. "That is a good sign. You're looking a lot better. I'll bring your breakfast up right away. Then I want to talk to you."

"And I to you," said Holroyd.

Tar had been withdrawing into the tunnel. He straightened. He eyed Holroyd narrowly, and said, "For a man who was nearly dead yesterday, you're taking a quick interest in life. What's on your mind?"

"I'll tell you after I've eaten," Holroyd replied cautiously. "It's in connection with something you mentioned."

"There's only one thing I've mentioned," said Tar with a surprising coldness, "that you in your position would be interested in: I told you that the rebels might find you useful because you claimed to be Ptath. That's it, isn't it?"

Holroyd was silent. He hadn't thought of this roly-poly, bouncing little man as having such a quick understanding, but it was his toughness that really shocked him. For the first time, he wondered what Tar was in jail for. He'd better proceed carefully. Tar was his one contact with the outside world.

"What about it?" Holroyd said.

Tar shrugged. "I'm sorry I mentioned it in the first place. Because it's off. They're not interested. They don't see how it could be worked in any practical fashion, and besides it would be too easy for you to vanish into distance. I'm being quite frank."

"But they *could* free me?"

The little man stiffened as if he recognized the depth of

will that was behind the quietly spoken words. His eyes studied Holroyd warily. He nodded finally, grudgingly.

"Good," said Holroyd. "Tell them to come and get me tonight."

Tar started to laugh. The laugh broke in the middle, instantly bridging the gap from sound into silence. He climbed out of the hole and scowled at Holroyd. His eyes were slitted, his lips a knife-thin line. Standing there, he seemed a small animal of a man tensing for action. He said in an ugly tone:

"That's a fine way for a fellow to talk after our organization has just saved his life."

The justice of the words stung. But Holroyd knew with an utter conviction that the morality behind them didn't apply here. This was different. Ptath, the thrice greatest, transcended any such confining ethics.

"Listen," he said earnestly, "the rebel leaders made their rejection blindly, without regard to my character or my personality, which renders their decision ill considered, lacking in imagination and, therefore, worthless."

He drew a deep breath and raced on: "Tell them I am prepared to play the role of Ptath on the largest scale, that if they are strong enough to seize this temple I am prepared to make it my headquarters. Tell them no army will ever gather recruits faster than the one that will swarm around me. Soldiers coming to attack will remain as my followers. I know enough to fool everybody including—" He stopped. He had been intending to say including the goddess. But so extreme a claim would not carry weight. He finished: "—including people of the highest intelligence."

"That's a lot of talk," said Tar coolly, "from a man who's in a dungeon."

"I was sick," said Holroyd. "Very sick."

Tar frowned, said, "I'll get in touch with them. It may take a week, though."

Holroyd shook his head. The prospect of a direct hostility between himself and Tar was not one that he relished. But there could be no evading the primes of his situation. While he still had several days' leeway, it would be madness to cut the time between his escape and the goddess' arrival too closely.

She would come. He was certain of that. She would come by the fastest transportation available.

"Tonight," he said flatly. "It's got to be tonight." His gaze fastened on the tunnel. "What about my escaping through there?"

There was no answer. Tar was lowering himself into the hole. As he ducked out of sight, Holroyd bent down, examined the bottom of the stone and then straightened, smiling grimly. A moment later Tar handed up some fruit, a glass of liquid and some bread. "Help me lower the stone," he said quietly. "I'll see what I can do for you."

Holroyd suppressed a smile. "I'm sorry," he said quietly, "but I've just noticed that there are notches in the stone for fastening it from below. I'll feel safer if the stone isn't replaced."

There was no answer to that either. One long, malignant glare Tar gave him, and then he was gone. But he came back; surprisingly he came back, with lunch, with supper. But he ignored Holroyd's advances with a studied silence that left no recourse finally but action.

CHAPTER V

Secrets Of A Temple

THE TUNNEL WAS A NARROW SHAPE OF DARK AND LIGHT. Tiny light sticks protruded from the ceiling, which was so low that Holroyd had to bend almost double as he walked. There were side passages, dark holes scarcely big enough for a man's body. Holroyd ignored them. It wouldn't do to lose his way in a labyrinth of byways. His only course must be to keep on this main corridor.

Curiously, Holroyd examined the first light stick. Like the others, it was made of wood. It felt cold to his touch, and when he pulled at it, it blinked out as if he had turned the switch. It was attached to the ceiling by a wooden hinge, but the light didn't go on again till he shoved the stick into contact with the concrete. The power must come out of the ground.

Holroyd was about to pass on when he noticed the tag hanging from the hinge. On it was written:

> Cell 17
> Occupant: Amnesia case.
> Remarks: None.

The tag on the second light said: "Cell 16, Name . . . Nrad . . . Made the mistake of hitting back at a temple soldier." Holroyd studied the laconic inscription with grim eyes. Nrad's mistake was one that he could appreciate.

At the end of the line of lights, in the darkness beyond cell No. 1, was a steep, narrow stairway. Holroyd climbed up it past dully lighted corridors, but it was the mental image that came that disturbed him, the picture of himself in this subterranean world of a temple that towered into the blue dark sky of an earth that had aged two hundred million years since his own birth. The time involved was meaningless, more alien than death. Funny how *pasts* meant nothing. There was only this climbing up a secret stairway in a half light, climbing—ten, eleven, twelve levels.

He reached the twelfth and last, searched with a brief intentness for an outlet that might take him to the roof, and finding none, stepped gingerly into the passageway and walked along it. The ceiling here was high enough for him to walk erect. But here as on the dungeon level were branching tunnels that he ignored on the same simple theory that, by moving in straight lines, he wouldn't get lost. Here too, were tags on every light. The first one read:

"Sadra, kitchen maid, pro-rebel, one of her lovers talkative Keep Sergeant Gan. Peephole but no entrance."

It proved a typical tag. Every room was occupied by a woman servant of some kind; most of them had lovers, most were rebel supporters—and every one that Holroyd peered in at was sound asleep.

The eleventh floor was occupied entirely by men servants, all sleeping. Soundlessly, Holroyd worked his way down the narrow stairway. Common zos occupied the eighth level, common fezos the seventh. The dark robes that hung over chairs and over the ends of beds identified them: priests! priestesses! The fourth level was the apartment of the temple prince, and, the general direction tag went on: "of his daughter, Giya, the temple princess."

Ambitious Giya, Holroyd thought savagely, cunning, treacherous, quick-thinking, power-covetous Giya. With clenched teeth, he peered through the peephole that was located at this end of her apartment. It took a moment to grasp the whole picture. In the immediate foreground of his narrow line of vision was a large, heavily carpeted room. There were settees, chairs, tables. At the far side was the open door of a bedroom; and it was there that real interest began.

The edge of the bed and a long, narrow, shining table with a mirror mounted on it, showed through the door. On a chair beside the table, at right angles to the door, sat the temple princess. Her lips were moving. Holroyd pressed his ear against the peephole. Formless words drifted to him, an unintelligible yet melodious monotony of sound. After minutes of watching, listening to that flow of sound, Holroyd left the peephole. Whoever she was talking to couldn't possibly matter as much as his search for a passageway to the screer pens, his need to fly off into the still dark universe of eastern Gonwonlane.

For a timeless period he prowled along side passageways, taking care not to venture too far afield. It must have been two hours later when he found himself again on the fourth level—and the temple princess was still talking. Frankly curious, Holroyd fumbled his way along the branch corridor that led in the direction of her bedroom. He stared in at her in amazement. She was alone. Her lips were moving, articulating; and her voice, as he put his ear against the tiny aperture through which he had peered, came strong and clear:

"—Let his minutes be days, his hours be years, his days centuries. Let him know endless time as he lies in the dark . . . His minutes be days . . . his hours . . . years—" Over and over the words were intoned; and at first Holroyd tried to think of them as a prayer, one of those endlessly repeated, senseless things designed to beat the mind into a pattern.

Then that first impression collapsed. Holroyd felt a mental dizziness, a daze of horror, an understanding at once comprehensive and as deadly as fleshed steel. What was she saying? *What was she saying?* 'Let his days be centuries.' Why, that's what they had been—for Ptath.

Too late Holroyd realized that his personal mind paralysis had briefly lost him control of his body to a mind that had no fear, no doubts. Even as he grew aware that his hands were manipulating the secret entrance to the room, the action was done; he was committed. He stepped through the opening and he must have made some sound because the woman came to her feet and turned with a tigerishly swift and inhumanly violent movement.

Funny, her appearance, Holroyd thought. He hadn't really looked at her body through the peephole. But then, he hadn't suspected. Hard to imagine just when the transformation had taken place. It must have been on the road, an attunement derived from the thought, the recognition of the god Ptath by the temple princess. The flash of recognition must have leaped across eight thousand three hundred kanbs to the distant city of Ptath and instantaneously brought the goddess to possess the princess' body. How it had been done was another thing entirely, impossible to explore now.

It didn't matter. He had betrayed Tar and the secret of the hidden passageways, and he felt a fury against the savage force inside him that was using his understanding and knowledge with such an utter disregard for danger and consequences. The anger ran its brief, futile course.

There was only the Goddess Ineznia.

She stood there, and she was different than Ptath's memory had pictured. From the memory, Holroyd had thought of a simple god succumbing to the deliberately displayed charms of the first woman who smiled at him. He should have known that Ptath would not be easily impressed by any human being, and at the same time would not be consciously aware of special qualities in those who did impress his untamed mind.

The woman blazed with life. No wonder the temple prince had frowned in amazement at his transformed daughter. Her eyes were pools of flamelike intensity; her body shed an aura as strong as blazing fire. Only her voice, when it came, was soft, though there was an eagerness in it, a strange passion and pride that, for an instant, had no relation to any reality.

"Peter Holroyd," she glowed. "Oh, Ptath, this is a great moment in our lives. Do not be alarmed by my recognition of your identity. Know only this, that we have tasted victory. We have won the first, though not the most dangerous round in the Goddess Ineznia's determined war to destroy you.

"She it was who drew you to Gonwonlane from the parallel time *before* you were due to come normally. Without knowledge, stripped of power, you were to be materialized in the citadel palace, and destroyed.

"Wait! Do not speak!" Her voice was suddenly as strong as a vibrating steel bar. Holroyd, who had parted his lips to express his bewilderment, closed them again. Not the goddess, he thought; this was *not* the goddess. The woman was pressing on, her voice more urgent:

"All those initial plans of hers I have frustrated. Using my carefully hoarded remnant of god power, of which she knew nothing, I placed you at this remote point of Gonwonlane, usurped the body of the temple princess, and placed your elemental mind under a constant strain of pressure designed to draw from its depth the whole personality of its last reincarnation. With success has this been done. And so, Peter Holroyd"—her tone was bell-like—"your fight for life begins. Act much as you would if you were in enemy territory. Be abnormally suspicious, but bold beyond all your previous conceptions on anything you decide to do. In crises trust your immortal body.

"Here is what you *must* do: You must conquer Nushirvan by any means that may occur to you. Think about that as you fly toward Ptath this night. It will take a little time for your mind to grasp the importance of this attack.

"And now"—she gave him a strangely sad smile—"that is all that I can tell you. Except for that, my lips are sealed by the same spell that has held my body in a dungeon of the citadel palace for more ages than I have been able to count. Ptath—Peter Holroyd—your second wife, long forgotten L'onee, will try to do more for you as the opportunity occurs, but now, quick, out onto my balcony and down across the courtyard to the screer pens and—"

Her voice trailed. Her eyes widened and flicked beyond Holroyd's shoulder. Holroyd half turned as the arrow from Tar's bow whisked past his head and buried itself in the woman's left breast. For a moment she stood rigid, then she smiled at Holroyd, a tender, eager smile. Holroyd caught her as she crumbled, heard her mumble:

"Just as well that this body die. It would remember—too much. Good luck!"

Behind him, Tar was shouting: "Hurry, man, get into these clothes. We're leaving right away." There were other cries in the vague distance, somehow galvanizing him.

As he ran his memory of her was of a rather plumpish young woman, from whom the flame of life had departed, lying very still on a thick rug. That memory remained sharp and clear until he was being pulled onto the back of a crouching screer by a dimly seen rider. The hammerlike beat of the windmill-like wings, the bang of the wind as the bird flew itself into the cloudy night sky crowded the picture from his mind. And then—

There was a wailing cry from the driver of Holroyd's screer. "I'm hit!" the man screamed. He seemed to throw himself forward on the back of the bird. When Holroyd reached forward into the darkness where the man had been, there was nothing but an empty saddle. A faint scream floated up from the night below.

He was alone on an uncontrolled screer in a strange, fantastic world.

CHAPTER VI

Flight Through
The Night

THE MOON CAME OUT FROM BEHIND AN ENORMOUS CLOUD. A great orb of moon it was, mightier than Holroyd had ever seen. It was very near, as if Earth and its silver, shining daughter had drawn closer to each other since the long-forgotten twentieth century. The lowering globe looked ten feet in diameter. It filled the night with radiance. By its light, Holroyd had his last glimpse of Linn.

The temple town shone softly in the moonlight that bathed it. The temple itself towered white and pure, like a pillar silhouetted in a light of its own. Around it spread the trees of the park, dark and strange. The first circle of buildings began just outside the park. Gradually, the scene receded into distance. The town became a misty shape on a vast, blurred land. That was the picture that stayed with Holroyd, the tininess of the town, the immensity of the land.

His mind let the town go. His attention withdrew from the past it represented, as it had deserted the woman earlier. He felt a sadness, a great melancholy. It struck him sharply that he had been striving all these minutes to push out of his mind the image of a human body falling down, down into the night. He was more shocked than he cared to admit. Death of companion and enemy he had seen often enough, but always there had been the knowledge in the case of the friends that he had no personal responsibility, and to hell with the enemy.

But this was friend, though personally unknown. And more than friend, a rescuer, who gave his life in the noble act. One more body, Holroyd thought darkly, one more shattered bit of flesh seeking its traditional and terrible union with the soil of earth. How many men had tumbled reluctantly from heights into that abnormal merging with the land? How many during two hundred million years?

The thought yielded to the rushing wind, the flapping of meaty wings, the night that seemed endless. Rage came against the darkness. "Damn you, Ptath, what are you trying to do—balance off seven hundred years in one night?"

It should be getting light, Holroyd thought blankly. Why, the temple's inhabitants had been asleep for hours, and he had been out here on this great airplane of a bird for yet more hours. But the night went on. Something was wrong, definitely wrong about this incredible flight through an endless darkness.

In the great rushing dark, Holroyd shifted uneasily in his saddle. L'onee, whoever, *whatever* she was, had said she would help him again. Was this some version of that help? It seemed hardly probable. Because she had also told him that he must go to the Nushirvan front to attack and destroy the outlaw State. Holroyd's mind poised there, ruefully. *He* must attack Nushirvan with its population of five billions, its endless mountains, its powerful and cunning fighting men. He laughed curtly. The harsh sound of his laughter was snatched from his lips by the whining wind, and lost in the vast night. But the thought remained; and after a moment he knew what she had meant and why it was possible.

In all ages a few men with wills of iron and personalities to match ruled, and made the decisions upon which the masses of their times built their lives. Very simply, very starkly, the demi-god Holroyd-Ptath must go to the Nushirvan front, take control of all the armies there and blitz Nushirvan before the Goddess Ineznia knew what was happening.

Holroyd drew a deep breath. He'd have to get in touch with the rebel groups, of course. And find out what the pamphlet Tar had shown him had meant in its statement that prayers were the source of the god power of the goddess. Because, if that was true, then where did Ptath derive *his* power?

Abruptly, he felt the immensity of what was here. The excitement of it clanged inside him. "A 1944 brain," he thought shakily, "dominating the body of the god of Gonwonlane." His consciousness lifted up to grasp at the wonder of it; his whole being blazed with sensational thoughts. And the strange long night lengthened.

Dawn came with tropical swiftness. The sun reared from

the horizon behind him and splashed its light across villages, farms, forests that had in their texture the shape of jungle. A green, prolific land it was.

Far to the north glittered a dark sea, and ahead was a city. The city was very far away, so vaguely seen that it kept fading into the mist of distance. There seemed to be a monstrous towering cliff beyond it. A cliff? Holroyd frowned. Ptath was the city of the great cliff, and no screer could possibly have flown a seven day journey in one night. Even as the denying thought came, Holroyd knew better. This was what the endlessness of the night had meant. Somebody was *pulling* him toward Ptath. Was it L'onee?

Abruptly, he knew that he couldn't even think of taking the chance. He had to force this beast down. Here. Now. This minute. He felt a sagging sensation. The next instant, like an enormous prey-bound hawk, the screer plummeted toward the distant rim of the jungle.

The land below seemed uninhabited. At the last moment Holroyd had a glimpse of a small, red-roofed house inset in a green shelter of spreading palm trees; and then the massive bird had flashed over the low line of jungle beyond. It came down in a clearing, ran at top speed, flapping its wings madly. As it came to a plunging halt, Holroyd saw for the first time the tufts of feathers on its ribbed, leathery neck. The sight struck him sharply, brought a ponderous wonder as to the screer's twentieth-century ancestor. But the development of flesh and bone was too radical; the physical structure would probably require the most detailed scientific investigation. But not by him who had never been able to recognize by sight more than a dozen birds. The reverie ended as a silvery voice spoke from behind him:

"You would be wise, Peter Holroyd—Ptath—to climb down."

Holroyd twisted in his saddle. A girl stood in a narrow pathway twenty-five feet away. There was a quiet earnestness in her dark eyes, a sadness in her olive-complexioned face, and a fire of personality that was unmistakable.

"Hurry!" said the voice of this new L'onee. "The flying screer does not linger long in one place untended. Be careful not to walk in front of it. It will not hesitate to peck at you.

Besides," she finished urgently, "we, you and I, Ptath, have but a brief hour together. There is no time to waste."

As he slipped to the ground, Holroyd experienced embarrassment. It was hard at first to determine the origin of the feeling, but after a moment he realized that it was her acceptance of him as Ptath regardless of the alien ego of Holroyd which had dominated the Ptath body now for hours. That domination was so complete that he could feel no difference. Ptath was Holroyd. It was a Holroyd, perhaps, who took the reality around him a little too much for granted; a Holroyd who might have been on his way to the Gonwonlanian equivalent of a madhouse if he had actually been in his *own* body. But, except for that, the merging of god and man into man was so thorough that even the god memory had a dreamlike quality. It was the supremacy of his personal identity that made the woman's intimate acceptance of him confusing as he walked slowly toward her.

She had not moved from her first position. Her eyes were dark and luminous. Her black hair hung down the back of her head in cascades, but it was not well brushed. Her face had the healthy prettiness of a country girl. Her well built body was definitely youthful. Holroyd saw that she was watching his survey of her, a faint, enigmatic smile on her lips.

"Pay no attention to this form, Holroyd," she said finally. "It is that of a peasant girl named Moora who lives with her father and mother a quarter of a kanb from here."

Paying no attention to her was easier said than done. She glowed with life. When she turned to walk along the trail her movement had in it such a springiness of youth, such an easy grace, that Holroyd stopped, fascinated. Hurriedly, however, he fell into step behind her, treading the narrow path wordlessly for several minutes. But at last he said:

"Where are we going? And what about the screer?"

She did not answer. They were deeper in the forest now. Trailing vines hung down from the trees. And so dense was the leafy foliage overhead that the long, slanting rays of the morning sun did not penetrate the gloom. It was a silent world of half light.

"How is it," Holroyd called, "that I reached the city of Ptath in one night's flying?"

"Wait with your questions," came the answer. "As for the screer, you need it no more."

They walked on. Holroyd thought of how the night just passed had lasted and lasted. His sense of danger increased; the consciousness that every passing minute could bring titanic surprise grew strong. Was he, who had been lured into a dungeon, following without question the woman who had lured him into it?

"See here—" Holroyd began. And let his words trail. The pathway, that had been so confining, was widening. A clearing spread out and there, a little to Holroyd's right, was the small building he had seen from the air. There was no sign of life. Over everything lay a profound stillness.

The silence extended to the house. It was a one-story structure, nice-looking, a design of skillfully cut wood. It looked neat, as if pleasant, wholesome people had lived there. *Had lived*. The deserted effect was relieved by the rug runner in the outer hallway. Standing on the threshold, Holroyd looked first at the alcove that opened at the right to what must be the living room; and then he looked slantwise at the girl.

"I am glad," she said earnestly, "that you are cautious about entering. But think! It was necessary that I trick Ptath into entering the temple dungeon in order that Holroyd might be reborn. As for the rest, be assured that I will go first wherever I ask you to go."

It wasn't, Holroyd told himself, that he had had any real doubt once she herself had entered, but why was he here at all? He shook his head dubiously. Then gave his attention to his surroundings.

The living room was scantily furnished. There were hard chairs, a rug, a chest, a table, a wooden light stick hanging from the ceiling, and in one corner on a dais a glowing metal bar. It extruded from the center of the dais. It shone with a dull violet radiance. Holroyd saw that the girl's eyes were following his gaze.

"A prayer stick!" she said.

Prayer stick! This then was the source of the Goddess Ineznia's god power. Holroyd moved toward the dais. How did it work? Just what did it do? He turned toward the girl curiously, and realized that she was still talking:

"Moora's parents are away and we are alone, Ptath, you and I alone for the first time in . . . in—"

She hesitated, then sighed. "The time," she went on wearily, "has no meaning. It is so long that I have died a hundred million deaths for need of you."

Her voice went on, more eagerly now, "Once more I shall be all women for you. Today, you can claim me as a peasant girl named Moora; tomorrow I shall be the beautiful girl from the silver city of Trinano, whom you see by chance in the street; the day after that a fancied lady of the court shall lie in your arms, and once more it will be really I, your happiest wife. Thus it was with us in the old days; so it will be again. Of course there is first of all this wretched business of Ineznia."

Holroyd hardly heard the last sentence. It was what she had said. The words quivered in his brain, the meaning of every syllable as distinct as the print in a book. The hard thought came that no blitz soldier should feel at a loss in a situation like this.

"But look here," he heard himself say, "do you mean to tell me that you actually used to take possession of other women so that—"

He couldn't go on. He saw that the girl was staring at him. A moue of disappointment wrinkled her lips.

"Oh, Ptath," she chided, "it is you who have changed if you find wrongness in what we did of old. You were the philanderer. I but yielded to your desire. It is your will and yours alone to which I shall conform always."

There was nothing he could say to that. The justice of the reproof was only exceeded by the strange pliancy of character revealed by the confession. A woman who catered to every abnormality of her husband's lusts. L'onee, Holroyd thought, L'onee, what feet of clay you have. No wonder your real body is lying enchained in a palace dungeon, prisoner to someone who looked at least a little bit beyond pleasure.

"Look," Holroyd said slowly, "you didn't bring me here just to make love to you. And, besides, I want to know how you did it. How did that screer fly so straight to where a peasant girl waited in a jungle clearing? Another thing," he pressed on, "that accident of the driver falling off the screer— *was* that an accident?

"Wait!" His voice was a resonant force. He waved violently toward the dais. "This prayer stick! How does it work? It seems to be made of metal, almost looks like steel. And the funny part of that, when I think it over, is that it's the first metal I've seen since coming to Gonwonlane." He finished, "Well?"

Her expression was quiet now. A shadow of a smile touched her eyes and then was gone. But Holroyd did not miss the faint amusement. Better watch out, he warned himself. This woman's character was undoubtedly more complicated than any single facet of her might indicate. After a moment she had still made no answer. She stood studying him; and it was curious, the intent expression in her eyes. As if she was considering his reaction to something that was still only in her mind. Abruptly, she walked over to the dais, from which protruded the prayer stick. She beckoned Holroyd, and there was a commanding note in her voice as she said:

"Take my hand, and I will show you how the peasants pray. It is important that you learn about this, as it is from the totality of billions of such sticks as this that god power is derived."

Holroyd shook his head. He had no sense of making an abrupt decision. The will, the consciousness had been growing on him, and now he knew that he was not taking another step forward that involved collaboration with anybody or acceptance of anybody's statements. He had been rushed along with a blinding speed. That was over. Above everything else he needed a few days to orientate himself, and plan his future actions. He grew aware that L'onee must have realized the reason for his reluctance. She came hurrying back to him.

"Don't be foolish," she said earnestly. "There's no time to waste. Delay of any kind might be fatal."

There was nothing to say to that. Beyond doubt dangers existed. It didn't matter. It was simply not in his nature to go on charging forward into the unknown. His silence must have seemed like hesitation. The girl, with an impatient gesture, snatched his hand and pulled at him.

"Come," she urged. "No matter what else you do, you must learn about this."

Her strength was surprising, but Holroyd disengaged himself with a quiet finality. "I think," he said, "that I am going to pay a visit to the city of Ptath before I do anything else."

He turned, and without a word, without waiting for her to speak, walked into the hallway and out of the house. Twice, while the tiny place was still visible, he looked back. But there was no movement, no sign of life. Silent as a house of evil, it stood in the light of the early morning sun and vanished from his sight as he plunged into the dense undergrowth.

CHAPTER VII

The Realm of Darkness

THE JUNGLE WAS WARM AND MUGGY, AND IT TOOK ABOUT AN hour of steady westward walking to break out of it. Holroyd stopped short. He had come into the open on a hillside and there was a long line of hills facing him, barring any view he might have had of the city of Ptath. To the north was a dark, glittering sea. But he scarcely noticed that.

It was the valley below that held his attention. The valley was a military camp. It swarmed with men and beasts and buildings—and women. The presence of the women puzzled him. But after a moment that wonderment cleared. Of course! This was a permanent encampment, with establishments for married men.

Maneuvers, or some kind of training, seemed to be in progress. He watched the unfamiliar pattern of action for a while. There seemed to be a lackadaisical quality about everything. The grimb-mounted cavalry galloped in a leisurely fashion, the riders carrying long wooden lances, and they had a habit of swerving their beasts out of line before a group of women, conversing for a minute, and then cantering off after the main body. It looked disgraceful, from a distance, though there was probably an explanation for it.

As far as Holroyd could see in either direction along the valley were soldiers and buildings to house soldiers, shining white in the sun. There was nothing to do but cross the valley. If he avoided Ptath's acquisitive tactics, he should be able to thread his way without even being noticed. He estimated the distance at five miles—an hour and a half.

He was about a third of the way across, passing quietly near a group of men and women, when there was a thunder of heavy paws. A long line of grimbs roared by within ten feet of him. Most of the riders looked at him curiously. But one man, a tall, fancily dressed chap, with colorful feathers in his alpine hat, stared in blank astonishment, then reined his great beast out of the line. He bowed low in his saddle.

"Prince Ineznio!" he cried. "Your unprecedented surprise visit will thrill the army. I shall inform the marshal at once."

He whirled away toward the nearby group of men and women, leaving Holroyd with a memory of what the temple prince had said on the road, that Ptath resembled, not only the statue in the temple, but a man called Prince Ineznio. Not until this moment had that vaguely remembered remark suggested danger.

Holroyd examined his situation with narrowed eyes. The valley was a world of movement of men and animals. There were buildings and soldiers behind as well as in front, and on every side of him. And coming toward him was a throng of officers and their women.

There was no way out, nothing to do but try to carry off the mistaken identity. If these people accepted him as Ineznio, he could learn from them the details of the army's make-up, and then—the Nushirvan front! He felt suddenly impatient with fear and caution, and an eager excitement. The details of the impersonation were not important. The almost certainty that his voice would not resemble that of Ineznio, didn't matter. He was Ptath, thrice greatest Ptath, *the* Ptath of Gonwonlane.

The identification clanged in his brain. With a savage confidence he watched as the group of officers and ladies reached him, paused, bowed low and waited, obviously for acknowledgment.

Holroyd gave it, ringingly, "I am here to see maneuvers, details of training. Let them proceed."

It was superbly done; only it was not Holroyd who had done it, but Ptath. No, not even Ptath exactly. It was the thought of Ptath's identity that had brought the arrogant response. Ptath was becoming more valuable, more integrated, every hour. He saw that the group, having been recognized, was at ease. The women were mostly young and good-looking; they eyed him with a frank interest. Several of the officers, one of them with ten white and five red feathers streaming from his alpine hat, came forward. The man was strong-faced, middle-aged; he said quietly:

"We are honored, lord. You will probably not recall our meeting at the palace when I was presented to you. I am Marshal Nand, commanding the 9430th reinforcement corps, which is shortly to proceed to the Nushirvan front." His voice went on, but in spite of all Holroyd's will to listen, he couldn't. The flush of Ptath's personality began to fade. His mind was bobbing like a cork in storm-tossed waters, at once stunned and absorbed. The nine thousand four hundred and thirtieth army corps. Back home an army corps comprised anywhere from forty to ninety thousand men. His own impression was that he had seen more than that in this green, luscious valley. But suppose it was the smaller figure. Forty thousand men in one corps out of nine thousand four hundred and thirty meant roughly ninety-four million times four— four hundred million men.

The shock dwindled. Actually, it was a small army for a country with a population of fifty-four billion. Nushirvan alone, with its five billion population, should be able to place one billion men on the field of battle. Holroyd drew a deep breath. There was a fascination inside him, a soldier's singing fascination at the military potentialities of such vast and terrible armies. He thought: They could be trained to blitz tactics, with screers as planes, and grimbs as tanks.

Every minute the tremendousness of this vast land was becoming more apparent—the importance of staying alive and living, actually living here, as he would have to do. Holroyd-Ptath, the god ruler of Gonwonlane—

"And if you will come this way, most high excellency," the marshal was saying, "I will have typical units perform for your benefit. Of the three hundred and fifty thousand officers and men in my corps—"

"Of the *what?*" said Holroyd. But he didn't say it out loud. He was aware of himself falling into step beside the heavy-faced marshal, his brain once more reeling out at a tangent. His original estimate must be increased ninefold. Thirty-six hundred million men not counting army corps above the 9430th. Here were nearly twice as many soldiers as there were human beings on the earth of 1944—the greatest army in the greatest land that ever was. *His* army, *his* land, if he could but grasp it; if he could but frustrate a goddess' schemes, a goddess' ambition, and take what was his.

Beside him, a woman's voice said softly, "I am here, Ptath, in a new body, to help—to advise—you."

The woman's words had a queer effect. They brought revulsion, a sense of having had unwholesome thoughts. Peter Holroyd, American, owning a world—damned undemocratic nonsense! But could he hope to defeat that strong and elemental Ptath part of him which had such aspirations? The doubt made him cold with anger as he twisted to glance at L'onee's new body. He calmed slowly. Her new form was that of a plump, middle-aged woman, and the selection interested him. Before he could speak. L'onee whispered again:

"I'm Marshal Nand's wife. His mistress is over there to your left. Ptath, the army must be transformed and reorganized. Ptath, women were not allowed in army training camps until a few years ago when Ineznia decided to destroy you. She wanted to make sure that the army was not in condition to launch the attack you would have to make on Nushirvan just in case you ever got into position to make it. But the rebel officers have resisted the deterioration, and so the army's basic condition is much better than she thinks."

"My dear," came the marshal's voice from the region of Holroyd's other shoulder, "you mustn't whisper to his highness."

"I was telling him something very important," the woman pouted. "Wasn't I, Prince Ineznio?"

Holroyd smiled, nodded. He felt suddenly immensely better. The smooth reply of the woman pleased him. This was life unfolding around him, moment by moment. L'onee's character had a lot in it that he didn't like, but she *was* trying to help him. He tried to picture all that that meant. She had said her true body was imprisoned in a dungeon. It was curiously hard to imagine the reality of that. He would have to rescue her, of course. Just how or when was as dim now as had once been the how of his attack on Nushirvan. He didn't even know where she was imprisoned. And she couldn't tell him.

Actually, the attack on Nushirvan wasn't any nearer. But it had been impossible. Now, a way seemed open, in the far distance of time. Perhaps a similar opportunity might occur in regard to L'onee's body.

"Ptath!" It was L'onee again. "You mustn't stay here any longer. You have seen all that is important. You know the main faults of the army, lack of discipline largely due to the presence of a mistress in every soldier's hut, a situation deliberately created by the goddess in her will to destroy you. Now that you know this basic truth, you cannot waste any more time here with one twenty-thousandth of the army that must be changed. I swear to you every hour, even every minute, is vital.

"Remember, Ptath, my body is lying in a dungeon darker than that which held you for such a brief period. If *she* should find my flesh untenanted, she could destroy it—and she would, instantly—and then only you, in your full strength, could again render me capable of being a pole of power. Ptath, for my sake as well as your own, let me take you to the next phase of what you must learn in your fight to save your life, and mine. Ptath, let me take you out of here through the realm of darkness."

Holroyd had listened to her uneasily, almost unwillingly, yet with the half conviction that he *had* seen the main faults of the army, and anything more could only be repetition with details. Now he stared at her in amazement.

"The realm of darkness?" he echoed.

She made an impatient gesture. "Merely a means of leaving this valley. What you have discovered here is something I would have told you before this day was out. Ptath, this morning is but begun, and yet a large portion of it has been wasted in your personal discovery of two facts: the defects of the army, and that Ineznio is a real person who resembles you utterly, even to the texture of his voice.

"I could have told you both facts in two minutes. Ptath, spend this morning with me, listen to what I have to say. Learn what I have to teach you. And then go to your destiny in your own way. Ptath, say that you will go through the realm of darkness. *You* have to say it. I am too weak to take you by force or I would do so instantly."

Holroyd hesitated, impressed in spite of himself. She was right. Of all his problems since his arrival in Gonwonlane, the greatest was his lack of information. His own reluctance to go on a conducted tour should not exclude a morning spent in question and answer. Perhaps he had been a little too hasty in leaving her so abruptly. Beside him, Marshal Nand said:

"Here we are, Prince. Please name the establishment you wish to see in action."

Name the establishment! Holroyd smiled ruefully. Yes, go ahead and name it. Give its technical name so that everybody would instantly realize his easy familiarity with the whole set-up. He faced the woman, whispered hastily:

"I will go through the realm of darkness. Now what?"

The answer was—reality.

At first there was only darkness. It was intense, impenetrable. Yet after a moment he knew that L'onee was beside him. His awareness grew sharper. Shadows, he thought, he and the woman were shadows flickering in the night.

How far?

The words touched his brain, though they were soundless and not directed at him. He couldn't understand that, just as he couldn't understand how he could catch her thought at all. It was very clear though that he was. His mind was sensitive beyond all human possibility; and he waited tautly with her for the answer.

The reply came from distance. All space and time sighed with that answering thought; echoes surfeited the infinitely black vortex, plunging in all directions faster than the shadowed shape of man and woman.

Farther, slave!

But the years are already long.

They will be longer. On, On!

The night of time deepened. Ages dissolved into the darkness, and the abysmal feeling came to Holroyd that eternity was as near as that all-enveloping night. He saw that part of the woman's mind was growing appalled. It was his first awareness that her consciousness was in two distinct sections. One portion writhed with impotent fury at the task her body was performing; the other portion was the slave, unresisting, dependent on that master brain somewhere out there in far space. The lightless paths of the universe rocked with the fears that burned in the servant part of her mind; that all was lost, that hope itself must die in this black nothingness; and her thought came harder, tenser:

How far?

Farther, fool!

But a hundred million years have we gone.

Farther, oh, much farther.

For a while, then, the woman's enslaved mind felt better, calmer, more confident. And the long night ended.

It was strange, the dream of darkness. Holroyd poised on the shadowed edge of consciousness, puzzled by the curious awareness that was in him. What had happened? He pushed feebly at the unsettling sense of oddness; pushed too, at the night that washed around him. Finally he opened his eyes.

He was not, as he had thought, lying down. His feet were firmly on the floor; and from where he stood he could see the peasant girl, Moora, standing facing him. His gaze flicked beyond her, around her, at the familiar scene of the living room of the cottage in the jungle, which he had left hours before. Holroyd's mind leaped with memory. Back here. She had brought him back here—through the realm of darkness. But how?

He said blankly, "Have I been dreaming?"

"It was a memory," said the girl.

That seemed to make no sense at all. Holroyd studied her, but the girlish face was expressionless. After a moment, however, she added:

"It was the memory of how Ptath was first brought to Gonwonlane. Only with your permission and during a transport period could I show you what happened. You will agree that it is worth knowing."

Holroyd stood still, running the picture, the memory, over in his mind. "But *you* were in it!" he said finally, and for a moment he had an enormous, almost an owlish conviction that he had picked a fatal flaw in the whole story. "In fact, you were the one who actually brought me."

He paused, remembering how part of her mind had been enslaved, the other part writhing in furious rebellion against the commands of that remote master voice. He heard the girl saying softly:

"Yes, I was in it, but not willingly. Perhaps now you have a clearer idea of the power that opposes you."

Holroyd nodded, and slowly an unpleasant thrill coursed along his nerves. Her explanation fitted with what he had experienced, but that realization was something to be accepted, and forgotten.

The woman, the *being* out there in space, who had

commanded. The Goddess Ineznia! There was no dismissing her. No longer was she just a name, but reality. For the first time, Holroyd realized that he was fighting for his life.

With deliberateness, Holroyd walked to the dais from which projected the prayer stick. Reaching it, he looked back at the girl, questioningly. Then he motioned at the stick. She nodded instantly and came forward. Her swift response made Holroyd smile ruefully. It was possible that he should apologize for having run out on her before just as she was about to illustrate with this very prayer stick the origin of god power. He decided not to. Because he had been right. Under the circumstances, knowing nothing, surrounded by strangeness his refusal to trust a stranger was justified. There was still risk, but it was dimmer, her good will proved by everything she had done. Beside him, the girl said:

"The prayer stick is important. But first I'd like to sum up for you the hard necessities of your existence in Gonwonlane." She went on, "You may have wondered why it is so vital for you to conquer Nushirvan. It is because of the Great Chair of Power. The chair was formerly at the citadel palace but—and note this well—it was moved because the moment *you* sit in that chair you will regain all your power.

"It was moved by Ineznia into the capital of the Nushir of Nushirvan with the Nushir's permission. Her belief is that she can destroy you before you can hope to reach it. Ptath, it is my opinion offered without qualification that only by invasion, using the largest, most powerful armies ever organized can you expect to reach the mysterious, nameless capital of the Nushir and claim the god chair of Ptath."

The girl paused, as if to give weight to every word, then with the utmost gravity:

"The time has come, therefore, for the most dangerous action. At all costs we must retain the initiative; and, as soon as I have shown you the meaning of the prayer stick, I shall explain what I think you should do next.

"Now take my hand."

Holroyd took her hand gingerly. It felt warm, almost tinglingly alive, as if the life force behind it had flame in it, an electric, vibrant fire. The thought came: what an experience it would be to kiss a woman who was so *alive!* He looked sharply at the girl. Had that subtle suggestion flowed from her mind along her arm? He decided it hadn't. He was perfectly capable of having such a thought all by himself. He watched with somber interest as the girl reached for the prayer stick with her free hand. Just as her fingers seemed about to touch, she paused and half turned:

"I would like to remind you most urgently that you resemble Prince Ineznio even to the texture of your voice."

"What," asked Holroyd, "has that got to do with—"

He stopped. He stopped because at that precise instant the girl's reaching fingers clutched firmly the violet-tinged metal bar. The fire must have plunged instantly through her other hand that was holding his. It was as if he was holding a live wire. Holroyd writhed with silent agony. He fought to break free. But there was no strength in his effort. All the strength was in the energy that poured into his body.

He had time to realize that once more he had been tricked.

CHAPTER VII

The Climber On
The Cliff

FROM WHERE SHE LAY HUDDLED ON THE DUNGEON FLOOR IN the palace, L'onee could still make out the form of the Goddess Ineznia. In the half light, seated in the great chair that Inezia had brought down especially days and days before, Inezia's small, finely shaped body showed moveless. The golden hair that crowned her head glittered faintly. She crouched there, her head drooped, her arms hung listless—her *essence* obviously still away from her body.

As L'onee watched that inert body, a pressure began to build up, as of a mind-wind blowing out of a vast night. Stronger it grew. Power flashed into the room. The lights that had been low, flared more brightly, revealed a man's body falling to the cement floor. The body landed with a soft thud. Simultaneously, the golden-haired woman in the chair stirred. She opened her eyes. She laughed.

It was a tinkle of sound, softly musical. Ineznia glided to her feet and stood above the dark woman. Her voice blazed with triumph:

"Ah, sweet L'onee, my plan is working. He thinks I am you, and he has already permitted me to take him through the realm of darkness. Accordingly, the most dangerous of the lesser spells, the necessity for showing him how Ptath was originally brought from the world of Holroyd to Gonwonlane, is now over.

"In addition he has felt the power flow of a prayer stick, not as Ptath originally planned, a direct flow, but strained through my body, divested of the two energies that were designed to stir his memory." Her laughter trilled, then faded as she said, almost as if she was calculating out loud: "I intend to keep him mentally off balance until at least three more of the spells are canceled. After that it won't matter.

There are several ways I can *force* him to cancel the sixth, aside from the attack on Nushirvan. As for the seventh, if I can ever get my hands on that chair for examination, I don't think Ptath will have to sit in it.''

She finished, ''I almost forgot, L'onee dear. I have included your name in a large list of people to be executed, which list he is going to be asked to sign. I don't really expect him to sign. The list has another purpose, to provide one more reason why he will consider the attack on Nushirvan imperative.''

L'onee stared at her tormenter with curiosity. The child face of the other was twisted with triumph. Ineznia's eyes were wide, her lips slightly parted. Passion showed in every contorted line of her expression, yet her face showed alertness, strength and capability. L'onee thought wearily: Two spells gone. Two of the seven canceled. She could picture how skillfully it had been done. Ineznia, posing as L'onee, gaining Ptath's confidence as she broke, one by one, the spells that protected him from final death. She forced an overtone of her old, threadbare sardonicism into her voice as she said:

''So you pretended to be me. Poor Ineznia! What a difficult role that must have been. And has he made love to you yet, Ineznia dear? Have you broken that Ptath spell?''

The golden woman shook her head. ''I don't mind telling you of my temporary failure. The fool is a moralist.''

''But so was Ptath, remember?'' L'onee's voice was richer, tinged with a malicious note. ''He would have none of your sneaking off into other women's bodies.''

She saw that she had struck fire. Ineznia was breathing heavily. Her eyes flashed a blue flame of anger. Then she laughed, bright, brittle laughter.

''What you do not seem to understand, L'onee, is that I have Ptath here in Gonwonlane ages before he would normally be due. And what is more, he is controlled by a human mind; a strong mind, to be sure, but one which cannot possibly adjust to Gonwonlane in time to interfere with my plans.

''He will wake up tomorrow thinking that I believe him to be my lover Prince Ineznio, and that *you* made the substitution in order to show him the urgency of an attack on Nushirvan. Not for long will he resist the psychological forces that I am preparing against him. As for the second spell, the necessity of Ptath recognizing my rights by making love to me—''

Her laughter came vibrant and confident. There was passionate determination in that burst of good humor. ''Do you think he will resist me, *me,* when we are alone in my apartment? He will think that his only hope while he is in the palace will be to keep up the pretense that he is Ineznio.

''Perhaps now you are beginning to understand why I have coddled that fool Ineznio all these years, even to the extent of allowing him the male form of my own name. His resemblance to Ptath's ever-recurring body made it immeasurably worth while.

''And now, L'onee, I must go. I am taking him to Prince Ineznio's apartment. There he will return to consciousness some time tomorrow morning. I'd like it even sooner than that, but I have been disturbing the fabric of time, and must now strive for balance.''

As she turned away, the stone door opened, and four men came in. They fell to their knees, bowed to the floor, then rose and picked up Holroyd's body. The goddess followed them to the door, then paused, turned.

''I want to warn you,'' she said softly. ''I have had to use you as a pole of power, and the result is that for the first time in ages you have a little power. Don't leave your body. I shall come back here from time to time, and if I find that you are absent I shall destroy your form. I need hardly tell you how fatal that would be for you. You would then be dependent on whatever power you still had, and that would gradually weaken. Eventually, you would not have the strength to leave any body that you might have entered, and would die with it after a prolonged period of agony.

''As you know, also, it is impossible for you to gain entrance to the flesh of any person in the palace without my being instantly aware—so govern yourself accordingly.

''One more thing!'' The smile on Ineznia's face was curiously earnest. ''I know that you have some vague hope that Ptath arranged his spells in such a fashion as to trap me. If I discover so much as one trap anywhere along the line—and I assure you that I will know instantly—I shall immediately destroy Ptath's present body and try again in his next reincarnation. But I shall not fail. I shall be the sole and eternal ruler of Gonwonlane. I leave you with this pleasant thought.''

This time she did not pause, but continued on through the door. Instantly the room was plunged into darkness.

For long, the dark woman lay almost blank-minded, conscious only of the damp stone and of the chilling weight of chains. A thought formed at last: Boastful fool, Ineznia! So he's in Prince Ineznio's apartment. And yes, Ineznia, you're right. I have a little power at last. Enough to kill him now, so that he can be born again.

It was hard getting out of her body, harder than she had expected. The strain of keeping that human form of hers alive was almost too much for her meager resources. The dungeon was too cold. Every minute of life, every degree of warmth, had to be fought for. But she was out, and aware of her body lying beneath her in a visionless blackness. For there could be no normal senses, no eyes, no ears, no touch, in this formless state, only that superb still-buoyant power that was the very core of her *essence*. Time was, long ago, when her body had remained controllable from a distance, when she was out. But the strength which made that possible had long since been drained from her.

Getting through the walls was easy enough. She knew the way. How often in the far past she had floated down that depth of cliff toward the distant, smashing waters to the whirlpool that tossed human suicides and luckless drowned ones like driftwood onto the rocky shore, only to carry them out to sea at high tide.

Slow, now! The sense of water was near and strong. Too strong. She must be too far out. She had the shore line finally, the water tugging at her from one side, the quieter land from the other. Twice, something else came in, a feeling of difference. But each time it was so feeble that death must have been there long ago.

And then—she had her body. Just how long the girl had been dead, it was impossible to say, but the aura of life that suffused from her countless still living cells was strong, almost coarse, compared to the gentle pressure from the sea and the land. L'onee hovered sightlessly. And then, she was in, her essence spreading out along the dead nerves. The body lay around her, resisting life with all the quiet strength of an inert mechanism. It was like moving in quicksand. Death for human beings was so final, so complete.

How long she lay there in that timeless night she could not begin to reckon. There *was* no time, nothing but this poor, racked body and the soothing restfulness of death.

Awareness of life came first in the vague throb of waters rumbling against a rock-pierced shore. Then there was a tingling that would have been pain except that she held it from her consciousness and waited. Slowly, she grew aware of the gravel and rock and sand pressing against her new body. Then came movement, legs yielding to sustained muscular pressure, arms twisting, a host of normal functions shattering the unmovement of death.

Sight came last. She saw the night, a distorted reach of cloud-filled sky and towering cliff. A ledge held her body between the cliff and the rippling chasm that was the sea; and there were other shapes of bodies. And there was the city of lights across the gulf. She fought off the nostalgia that sight of the city brought, and forced action from her resisting limbs. For a while, she stood swaying, half slumped against the cliff that loomed so immensely into the night above her. And the thought came that no human muscles could ever hope to climb that fantastic precipice.

But shirking was not possible. She must kill to save. She found the weapons where she had hidden them during those occasional melancholy trips when, tiring of her dungeon, she had walked along this rocky shore where so many drowned people paused for a mindless rest before being swept out forever to the ancient sea. How long ago, now, seemed that last walk!

She powered the weapons and began to climb. The night dragged. The clouds drifted over the sea to the northwest. For a while the stars shone down on her where she strained against the gigantic height of the cliff. A sudden wind whirled in crazily. The clouds came racing back, blacker now, as if they had gone to the source of rain with the one purpose of coming back to torment her. The rain came down heavily. It washed her face, and did wet, cold things to her arms and body. When it ended finally, the dawn that emerged from the bank of clouds was already well advanced.

The sun came up in a blaze of red into a haze-filled horizon. There was distance below her now, but still the titanic precipice stretched on above, unconquered, demanding yet more strength, more endurance from her weary body. Death for the man—their only hope—seemed a long, long way off indeed.

CHAPTER IX

The Citadel Palace

FOR HOLROYD, THERE WAS NO SENSE OF TIME PASSAGE. ONE instant he was struggling against the energy that flowed with such appalling violence through his body from the hand of the girl; the next instant, awareness came that he was lying on the floor of a large room—a strange, sunlit room.

It was two hundred feet long and a hundred feet wide, at least, but after a moment he had no sense at all of dimensions. There was only an overall exquisiteness, an emanation of splendor that was shared even by the pattern of windows on the curving expanse of ceiling, through which sunlight streamed.

The furniture glowed at him, flame-patterned rosewood, the chairs and chesterfields and settees full-fashioned, with beautifully woven, matching cloth. The paneled walls shone with the soft blue of some amazing treasure wood. At the far end of the remarkable room was a series of gemlike doors, set in a design of stained glass windows. Through these windows, too, the sunshine poured, and there was an illusion of trees beyond—illusion because at that distance, even the clearest portions of the stained glass did not show a good picture of what was outside.

In a maze of fascination, Holroyd started to sit up, then slowly sank back again, stunned by the picture the movement brought into his line of vision. Coming toward him was the most exquisite thing in all that marvelous room, a golden-haired young woman. Just as he had had no time really to observe the room, so now his first impression of the woman was confined to a swift glimpse of intense blue eyes and a slender body encased in a form-fitting, snow-white robe; and then her voice came, sweetly urgent with anxiety:

"Ineznio!" she said. "What happened? You fell over like a stunned Vrill."

She stopped, and Holroyd had time to focus his mind on one facet of the series of events. Ineznio! His mind clung to the name. He thought in agony: "She's put me in the palace, substituted me for Prince Ineznio."

Memory came of what L'onee had said, that the time had come for dangerous action. Comprehension fanned the flame of his courage. Momentarily, still, he felt dazzled by his situation, then he grew confident. He said:

"I tripped. Sorry."

He stood up. The young woman's soft white fingers helped him. She was strong. Like a tigress, Holroyd thought as he watched her walk away from him toward, not the glass doors but one of several opaque wall doors. She stood in the open doorway silhouetted against a marble hallway beyond; and she said:

"This morning Benar is going to bring you the lists of those to be executed. I hope that you have now made up your mind to sign them." Her blue eyes blazed. "It is my will that we make an end of these so-called patriots whose only purpose is to force Gonwonlane into a war with Nushirvan and, later, with Accadistran. I shall return to discuss this further."

She was gone. Holroyd put up his hand as the door closed, as if the action would somehow call her back; as if the movement would conjure up an explanation of what she had said—*lists* of those to be executed. After a long moment his mind was still blank. L'onee had put him into the palace, substituted him in the most dangerous fashion for Prince Ineznio. Why? To prevent the executions? Or simply to let him see how vital were the life-and-death matters that hung in the balance. Only one thing was clear. He was on his own inside the citadel palace.

Holroyd paced the carpeted floor. His immediate purpose, it struck him finally, must be an apparent acquiescence. He had to find out all there was to know about this situation before mapping out his plan of action. His pacing brought him near the doors at the far end of the room. He peered through. The varicolored glass softened the brilliant sunshine that poured down on a terrace bright with flowers, on the trees and grass and shrubs that spread beyond; and beyond that again appeared the muted outlines of a city.

Holroyd flung open one of the doors and stepped through.

A breeze blew across the terrace. It caressed his cheeks and brought the fragrance of a garden in bloom, and there was a tangy smell of salt water. But it was the city that drew his eyes. The part that he could see ran along the shore of a blue-green ocean; and the whole glittered at him, a vision seen through a shifting network of design, like pieces of a jigsaw puzzle, through the green foliage of the trees. He hesitated no longer, but hurried across the terrace and down the wide steps to the greensward, and along the mossy bank of a brook that bubbled out of the ground and gushed under an avenue of trees. ·

It was the abrupt ending of the brook that brought Holroyd up short. The water simply gurgled, ran over a rocky ledge and vanished. He went cautiously forward, stumbling through underbrush. There was a garden walk of the same substance as the terrace, there was a stone railing about three feet high, and an abyss.

The precipice started just beyond the barrier of stone and fell down, down, down. Holroyd could see the path of the brook as it cascaded into that astounding depth, half a mile at least. Never was an abyss more accurately called the Great Cliff. At its remote bottom was a rock-strewn tongue of sea. No harbor would that bay ever be, for the thunderous roar of the lashing water came faintly to his ears. The water raced, in foaming masses, between two rocky points from the vaster ocean beyond, and formed the bay. A mile, two miles, three miles wide it was; and on that opposite shore the city began.

The sea and the cliff that enclosed its fury took their places in the intricate pattern of impressions that was forming in his mind. But for the moment there was only the city. It was white and blue and green and red and yellow and a myriad merging colors. It shone like a jewel splitting the rays of the sun, only not like that at all. It was a vast spread of cupolas and domes and steeples that blurred toward the distant horizon. It curved along the shore of that blue, enormous body of water, of which the untamed bay was but a tiny projection, curved into distance. There was a vague blur of forest beyond; and somewhere out there must be the cottage in the jungle from which he had been projected. Holroyd laughed curtly. He'd have to watch out for that woman L'onee. Twice now she had lured him into danger.

The arrow struck the stone beside him, poised for a moment like a live thing, then fell slowly, but with gathering speed back into the abyss from which it had come. Holroyd stared after it. He shook his head, puzzled; and then, just in time, he saw the figure on the little ledge fifty feet below him and to his left. He ducked as a second arrow split the air where his head had been. He half staggered back. But that one swift glimpse of his attacker had shown a tall, gauntly built young woman.

Once the first shock was over, Holroyd's alarm faded. He peered cautiously over the stonework, and saw that the woman was clinging precariously to some dark roots that wormed their way out of the perpendicular wall. The bow that had twanged at him so viciously was slung now over a bony shoulder. There was a belt around her waist with a sheathed sword hanging from it. As he watched, her fingers groped for new leverage, and so tense was the action, so great her danger, that Holroyd instinctively tightened his muscles and pulled with her.

He called, "Who are you? What do you want?"

His answer was the raucous scrambling noise and the gulp of labored breathing as the woman clawed foot by foot toward him. Holroyd felt suddenly isolated. He had an uneasy sense of aloneness, of one man against a whole strange world. The city across that darkly writhing bay seemed remote in space and alien. Involuntarily, he glanced back toward the palace. He could see only flashes of it through the green profusion of garden, a long, low, white building. Nowhere was there a sign of movement. Not a sound issued from it, not a quiver of life. Like an old and lifeless relic from forgotten ages, it stood there high above a restless sea. Old and dead. And only he and this woman who had tried to kill him were real and alive.

He saw that the woman was resting, one arm entwining a thick root. She looked up; and her face, tilted toward him no more than sixteen feet away, looked so horrible that Holroyd shrank. The woman called to him in a harsh voice:

"Don't mind my appearance. I'm ill from my long climb. And please, you must accept my apologies. I didn't recognize you. I thought I had been discovered by a guard."

Holroyd half smiled. The physically immortal Ptath need

not worry about arrows. The problem was to find out why this assassin wanted to kill Prince Ineznio, and why she thought an apology would make any difference. He watched her as she labored toward him. At ten feet she was a dirty, ragged, wretched-looking creature. Her straggly hair was mud-caked, her gray shorts and blouse were splotched with grime from the rocks and the spray from the foaming waters beneath her. The overall effect was of somebody at the end of physical strength. Holroyd frowned. What was he going to do about her? He couldn't take the risk of her firing at him again. Ptath's body might be invulnerable, but he did feel pain. As the woman reached the ledge just below the stone wall, he said quietly:

"Better drop the bow and arrows and the sword down the cliff. I can't let you come up with them. For your own sake do it quick and I'll give you a hand up."

The woman shook her head. Her voice blazed with passion as she answered: "I won't give up the sword. I'd rather jump off the cliff than fall alive into the hands of the palace police. I'll give you the bow and arrows. That way you can keep me at a distance. But the sword I keep."

He couldn't argue with such intensity. He took the shakily extended bow and arrows and after a minute of straining, jerked the young woman up beside him. No animal could have been faster than she, or more cunning. She started to collapse toward the stone walk. But the action was a ruse that covered the drawing of her sword, the instant lunge of her body toward him.

Holroyd leaped back, and in his surprise dropped the bow and quiver of arrows. She snatched them as she leaped after him, flung them over her shoulder back toward the cliff. They fell out of sight into the abyss. And then she was upon him. Her bony body twisted as she thrust her weapon. The lunge missed as Holroyd whipped aside. He had firmer control of his feet now. But, astonishingly, she was quicker than he. She hurled herself past his clutching fingers with utter abandon. Even then she would have missed except that, at that moment, Holroyd became aware of a startling fact. Her sword was made of varnished wood. *Wood!*

The realization that even such a weapon was not made of metal slowed him. The point of the stave caught him on the right breast. The pain was insignificant. It was instinct, not purpose, that made Holroyd snatch at the blade. He caught it halfway from the hilt and with a single jerk tore it from her fingers. He grew aware that the woman was staring wildly at the weapon. She mumbled:

"The magic stave—it doesn't harm you."

"The *what!*" said Holroyd. Then he realized what she meant. The sword blade tingled in his fingers. It was alive with a kind of inner movement. It vibrated like a machine-driven tuning fork. It warmed, then burned his hand with its pulsations. It felt exactly, in a much smaller degree, the way L'onee's hand had felt as she touched the prayer stick. Holroyd dropped it as he would have a hot coal. Before he could recover himself, the woman snatched the stave from the ground and flung it out over the precipice. She whirled to face Holroyd.

"Listen carefully," she said. "The stave should have killed you. The fact that it didn't shows that some of the women out there"—she waved her hand to the far horizon, south and east—"are praying to their prayer sticks. A pitifully small number, but", her tone grew thoughtful, "considering the immense time that has elapsed since women were first forbidden to pray except through their husbands, it seems to offer a hope. Ptath, you must think about that. You must—"

"Ptath!" said Holroyd. Until this instant he had stood striving to hold his mind tight around the idea that the woman thought he was Prince Ineznio. He had wondered how Ineznio should be taking her words. Her identification of him echoed in that dreamy garden with a fateful vibrance.

A stranger knew his secret, and suddenly that seemed so catastrophic that the shock of it was like a neural explosion that stabbed into his brain. He stared numbly at the woman and the look on his face must have been an unnatural thing, for she said quickly:

"Don't be a fool. Killing me won't help. Pull yourself together, and listen: I—might—be able—to help—you. Not here, not now. I must leave the palace. So if you will give me an order on the screer pens—" She finished: "The order blanks are in your apartment. Just follow me."

Holroyd followed. He had the feeling that this was a dream, this woman who knew him, who had tried to kill him and who now was quite blandly, and correctly, assuming that he would let her go without a word of protest.

He watched somberly as the woman slipped with easy familiarity through a door into an adjoining room. She emerged with a sheet of stiff, embossed paper, a curious glass-pointed, long-handled pen and a dull metal ring.

"You'd better put this on," she said, extending the ring. "It's the great seal of Prince Ineznio, and gives you authority second only to that of Ineznia herself."

Holroyd suppressed an impulse to deny her identification of him, her casual assumption that, beyond all doubt, he was not Ineznio. It was too late for denials. He took the ring. He found himself noting meticulously that she had referred to the goddess by her first name. He thought: "Who is she?" Not L'onee. Her personality was too human, so much less dramatic, and besides her actions were at wild variance with the whole scheme of things L'onee.

The woman finished writing. "Press your ring here," she said quietly.

Holroyd obeyed without a word. He was thinking of the danger that was here, a woman who knew his secret, at large. He would be a million times safer if someone would take her out and shove her over the cliff. One thing he was sure of, he couldn't let her leave without finding out who she was and what was her purpose. He picked up the document, and held it away from her reaching fingers. He was parting his lips to utter the first question when a sharp knock sounded on one of the opaque corridor doors.

As Holroyd turned with a start, he felt the paper snatched from his fingers. He half whirled, made a grabbing gesture. But the woman was running swiftly toward another of the corridor doors. She flung it open. Holroyd had a glimpse of marble corridors beyond, and then the woman was pausing, turning. She stood there, silhouetted, a tall, gaunt, ungainly female dressed in ragged shorts and shirt, with bare, mud-discolored legs. She said:

"I'm sorry, Ptath, that I can tell you so little. My lips are sealed, so sealed that . . . that—" She seemed to have difficulty with her voice, for she almost choked. When she spoke again her tone was more earnest. "Ptath, she is more dangerous than any of her present actions or words can possibly indicate. Beware!

"Ptath, whoever you are, whatever the identity of your ego, if you can recover the full power of the godhood of *the* Ptath, it will be your power. Yours to do with as you will. Of all the things you must do, recover that power first. Think of noth—" Once again she seemed almost to choke. She shook her head, tried again, then smiled wanly. "You can see," she finished, "that I won't be much help to you—here. Good luck, Ptath." The door closed behind her.

Holroyd could hear the knocking on the other door again. He felt impatient with it, a sense of being irritated by petty matters. It took a moment to realise why it was whoever was knocking didn't matter. He was Ptath. For the first time since coming to the palace, actually for the first time anywhere, that knowledge had been brought home to him in a personal way. Holroyd was Ptath. Any victory that materialized for Ptath was *his*. He must win. He had a sudden thrill of tremendous destiny that ended as another knock sounded. He shrugged. "Come in," he said.

A tall, powerful woman carrying a spear entered briskly. She presented the spear before her face and clicked the heels of her hard sandals. She said, "The merchant Mirow, great Ineznio. He says that the goddess herself has sent him to you. Shall I admit him?"

Holroyd stood cold, becoming colder, steelier. His indifference was almost a concrete force. A merchant. In projecting him here, L'onee must have known there would be Mirows. She must have meant him to meet them, to learn something from them. He would learn.

CHAPTER X

The Book Of Death

THE COMING OF MIROW BEGAN WITH THE SOUND AS OF A bellows wheezing through a faulty nozzle, the sound moved from some hidden point beyond Holroyd's line of vision, heaved obscenely nearer, and revealed itself as the stentorious breathing of an enormous, ugly-fat man. The human barrel waddled through the door, bowed from the waist with an elephantine grace and said servilely:

"Great Ineznio!"

Holroyd stared icily. "Well?"

The change that came over the creature was amazing. The politeness dropped from him as if it had been a mask, as if he had received permission to reveal the personality that quivered behind his beefy face. He closed the door through which he had come; then, like some great slug, he sidled over to Ineznio and a whine came into his voice as he almost blubbered:

"My lord Ineznio, you are a hard man to get hold of. I've had the Zard's treasure here for three days. I met the goddess in the corridor just now. Her divinity said you'd fix me up today. Can I count on that?"

"Yes," said Holroyd. He felt remote, uninterested. It didn't matter what it was, or why. He couldn't possibly gather enough details in an hour or a day to add weight to any decision. He saw that the bulbous creature was bowing and smirking. The fat man said:

"If you will accompany me to the Hall of Commerce, and put your seal on the delivery scroll in the usual manner—"

There was a corridor where women soldiers stood with spears guarding doors, then a huge white room where a score of men carried sacks to a great stone weighing machine. There were other men, one with a long nose, close set eyes, and an oily manner, who said:

75

"This way, your most high excellency. As soon as you are seated we will begin."

The men kept dumping the contents of the sacks in front of him; rough pieces of dark-brown metallic substance that was, he saw, raw iron. Brief interest came to Holroyd. Iron a treasure. Then his observation had been correct. Gonwonlane was metal-starved, what there was—used for religious purposes, for the vital prayer sticks that kept alive the goddess' power. In two hundred million years wasteful man had exhausted the ores of his planet.

He said to Mirow, "Where is the scroll receipt you mentioned?"

It was the vulture-countenanced man who brought it. The fellow presented it with a bow: "Oh, most high lord Ineznio, it must be wearying for one of your station to follow such routine. I shall see to it that we get the full measure of our iron."

Mirow, annoyingly, followed him to the door. "I shall have my messenger tell the Zard that you promised—Ah, here is Benar, the war minister. He will be as pleased as the Zard. Greetings, Benar."

Holroyd nodded at the elderly, corpulent man who bowed low to him. Part of his mind was thinking: One more of a thousand such as Mirow, to be accepted with awareness. The old fellow had petulant lips, sagging cheeks, and there were black pouches under his eyes. Meeting him was as drab as meeting Mirow and the laborers and the long-nosed vulture of a man. Only an alert, intent portion of Holroyd's mind tightened over the words that Mirow had spoken: The Zard of Accadistran would be pleased—about his promise.

He found himself frowning over the puzzling factors involved as he walked beside the old man who chattered insistently in a low falsetto. Treasure from the Zard of Accadistran who, according to the rebel pamphlet Tar had shown him, was responsible for the outlaw depredations. Treasure in return for a promise—Beside him Benar's voice grew harsh and blustery; penetrated:

"I'm glad you've agreed. Kill the whole gang; that's the only method."

"Eh?" said Holroyd sharply. "What was that?"

The old man looked at him, then, pompously said: "A

surgical operation, that's what's needed. I've got the list ready, every officer who ever spoke twice in public in favor of an attack on Nushirvan—this'll wipe them out. It's the only effective way to carry out your promise that our troops won't interfere when the outlaws employed by the Zard come over and abduct those scoundrelly rebels and their families.''

For Holroyd, high disinterest faded. He grew conscious of a purpose. It wasn't clear. So vague it was, in fact, that it seemed more like a vast unease; the will to action of a man who in pitch darkness has come up against an unscalable wall with passage possibly only through total destruction.

He was led into a large room. Maps hung on the walls. He recognized them: Gonwonlane, Nushirvan, Accadistran—it was all there, in much greater detail than the books had shown. But he gave them no more than a casual glance. He sat down and stared at a book the size of a large office ledger that lay on the desk before him. It was good to be sitting, for it made possible a mental summation about—a Zard who sent treasure—in return for the right to kidnap Gonwonlanian citizens—without interference from troops—the stupefying treason of a goddess against the people she ruled. He felt cold and deadly and without anger. This was what L'onee had meant. This was why he was here. She had thought he didn't comprehend the importance of the attack on Nushirvan. And it was true. He hadn't. The man Benar was speaking:

''As you can see, a large list. We didn't miss a single suspect.''

The comment, Holroyd suspected, was designed to draw a compliment. The list, the war minister's manner suggested, deserved praise for its very size. The man looked smug. His eyes glowed expectantly on Holroyd.

Holroyd flipped the book open, approximately in the middle. The page thus revealed was covered with almost microscopic writing—seven, eight, nine, ten columns of names. He counted one column with all the preciseness of suppressed emotionalism—forty names to each column. That meant four hundred to the page. He leafed the page over and sighed gently. It was written on the other side also, just as finely, with just as many names. It would be interesting to know the number of names. Not that it mattered. The mass murder that was contemplated here could not possibly gain by any reduction to exact figures. Nevertheless, he put the question.

"Eighteen hundred pages," the old man replied. "I tell you, sir, we've been thorough. We'll stamp this disloyalty out utterly."

Four hundred times eighteen hundred, Holroyd thought painfully. Four hundred times . . . times— The answer wouldn't come. Eighteen hundred by four hundred—no, that wasn't the way things were measured; sixteen inches by ten inches by four. Six hundred and forty cubic inches of dead men. Holroyd reached forward gravely and lifted the volume. Heavy, about eight pounds. It was the heaviness of the book in his fingers that brought the thought. He said:

"I'll take the book with me." He felt quite casual. "There are a few names, you know, that I must check to make sure they're not on it. It will take a little time to recollect them."

He was turning away with the conviction that everything was explained when the man's voice stopped him. "I assure you, sir, the lists were very carefully checked against the names of all officers who have been introduced into high circles, or otherwise called to your attention. Only such agreed-upon names as General Maarik, Colonel Dilin and others were left in."

"Nevertheless," Holroyd said freezingly, "I'll take the book to my apartment. I will study it there." He turned and walked into the corridor and to his apartment. He was closing the door behind him before he saw the golden goddess.

She was sitting at a little table that had been set up just inside the great stained windows. The table had dishes on it. The goddess said:

"Sit down, Ineznio. I want to talk to you about the executions. The minister of police made a suggestion a while ago that fascinates me. As a result I am thinking of sending you to the Nushirvan front to launch a false attack there that will satisfy all the malcontents. But sit down, my dear, and we shall discuss the campaign over a cup of nir."

CHAPTER XI

The Ring Of Power

IT TOOK TIME FOR HOLROYD TO ADJUST TO THE PRESENCE OF the goddess, and to her words. His mind started from almost blankness, and kept twisting away from the reality she represented. But it came back. It came back.

Seeing her now was different. Before he had been stunned by the ruthless manner in which he had been projected into her presence. And her own swift departure had left him with only a fleeting impression. Looked back upon, his arrival in the palace seemed like a sketch drawn on a hazy day, needing details to fill in the accurate general picture. The child's face, the small, finely shaped body, the blue eyes—all were much as he remembered. In place of the white negligee, the goddess wore a trailing gown of deep blue that matched the color of her eyes. But the great difference was that before she had seemed a dreamlike figure. Now she was real. She was alive, here, the Goddess Ineznia.

Her voice came softly, "Sit down, Ineznio. You're very strange this morning, staring at me so thoughtfully."

"I'm thinking over what you said," Holroyd heard himself say. Actually, he hadn't reached her words yet. But the answer sounded right. He seated himself gingerly and saw that she was regarding him with eyes that held an enigmatic, unchildlike quality in their depths. It seemed to change her appearance subtly. He found himself striving tensely to discover just what was the form of that new difference. And couldn't.

Realization came more sharply this time that he was staring at her again. He thought: Watch out, you incredible idiot. This is not just a woman. But it was hard to grasp that, harder still to follow its implications, except— Watch out! The cautioning thought brought a vague quaver of alarm, the knowledge that he couldn't go on being "strange", and that he mustn't remain silent any longer.

"So you would like me to launch a fake attack on Nushirvan?" He couldn't go on. For the first time he realized what she had said. He grew quiet. He could almost feel himself absorbing the possibilities. He thought finally: "It could be so easy."

The goddess was saying in a bell-like voice:"—I will send the messengers announcing that you and your staff will leave for the front tomorrow. All temples will be commanded to hold their forces at your call, and to prepare for housing and handling of transient soldiers. The great central stock of food and munitions will start moving to the front by every available means. The important thing in launching the attack is to convince everybody that a vast war is being waged, and at the same time to make sure that the known rebels are assigned to the left flank, where they can be cut off by the outlaws, and destroyed in the volcanic marshes and mountains that dominate hundreds and hundreds of square kanbs in that region. But I will show you in a minute exactly what I mean—"

Holroyd heard every word, but not too clearly. He sat in a gentle, personal haze of mind. There was joy in him, and dislike so violent that it hurt his mind. There was an icy rage, and there was pleasure. The pleasure came last because the other emotions promised to be more permanent, but they couldn't match in intensity the diabolic happiness that grew out of the proposal she was making: A false attack on Nushirvan. O Diyan, O Kolla. O divine Rad! An attack on Nushirvan under the auspices of the goddess, the necessary preparations made without arousing any suspicions anywhere.

The thought trailed. A slim white hand with pointing finger was reaching across the table toward his head. "Come with me," the goddess voice caressed, "and I will show you." The finger hovered above his forehead. "Hold your head steady, and come with me."

His impulse was to jerk back from he knew not what. But he didn't dare. He had time for a bitter consciousness that he should have remembered that this was a goddess, a goddess possessing power so great that even L'onee, who had been able to distort the very fabric of time, was terrified of her. The finger touched his forehead.

Come with me!

There was no change. The goddess looked at him, the firm, creamy flesh around her eyes drawn into a frown. "That's strange," she said. "I feel resis—" She cut the words with a deliberate click of her tongue. She sat back then and stared at him in astonishment.

Holroyd found his voice. "What's the matter?"

"Nothing, nothing." She shook her head impatiently, and it was as if she was trying to convince herself.

Holroyd waited. What she had expected to happen wasn't clear. But the reason why it hadn't, was. Dim might be the power of Ptath, compressed now into the personality of Peter Holroyd, but that intimate combination of human and god could not be treated as all human. Whatever she had meant by commanding him to come with her, wherever she had willed that they go, taking Ptath there and taking Ineznio must, by the very nature of things, involve *different* applications of her god power. He was about to be discovered. He felt hot, then cold and terribly steady.

"Ineznio, what have you been doing since I saw you last?"

The words were sharply spoken. Her eyes were glittering at him with a sparkling intensity like dancing blue water caught by a complication of sunbeams. It was hard to look at her. Her face seemed lost in a mist of light; light that pulsed and leaped. It seemed to have no source, but grew out of the air around her.

"Since you last saw me!" Holroyd echoed, and his tone was so cool that he felt a thrill. "Let me think! First," he began, "I went out into the garden. Returning I found Mirow waiting to see me. I went with him to check the Zard's treasure; then—"

He stopped. Her eyes had changed again. They were round, cerulean pools shadowed like the sea under a sky that had clouded, but with electric-blue sparks in their depths. And those eyes were staring now, not at his face but at his hand. His left hand.

"Who gave you that?" she asked in a piercing tone. "*That* ring?"

"The ring," said Holroyd. He stared at the dull shape too

astounded for a moment to say more. He caught his faltering thought. He began: "Why, it's just—"

He was cut off by laughter. A tinkle of sound it was, and the woman's finely molded, amazingly youthful face grew warm and alive with the rippling play of that delicious laugh. There was only one thing wrong. Her eyes had changed again. Still blue they were; but fire-blue now They blazed with a hellish, an unhuman rage. And her voice had in it the violence of sea storms, the lashing devil-vibrance of the elements. She screamed:

"Who gave it to you? Who? Who?"

"Why, Ineznia!" said Holroyd mildly. He felt shocked, but more than that, he felt in control of the situation. He stared at her curiously, genuinely interested. "It's really very simple," he went on, and knew with certainty that Holroyd alone could never have been so calm, so reasonable, so fantastically brave in the face of her demoniac outburst. "I was on the point of going out with Mirow," he explained, "when he reminded me I didn't have my seal ring on. In my hurry I must have picked up the wrong one."

It sounded semiplausible. The ring must have been there, in the room from which the gaunt woman had secured the order forms. Though why such a dangerous ring had been given into Prince Ineznio's care was another matter. He saw that the remarkably expressive eyes were changing again. Still blue, but they were steady now. As abnormally steady as was he himself. And her voice, when it came, was calm and quiet:

"I must ask you to forgive me, Ineznio. There are forces at work, of which I have not informed you, and I have recently been frustrated in something of great importance. Remove the ring, and then I will take you on a journey of minds. Afterwards—" She smiled, an amazingly tender smile, said softly, "Afterward I shall say good-bye to you in a manner befitting the separation of lovers. But first, put the ring away—back where you got it."

Holroyd walked slowly into the room from which the gaunt woman had brought the ring. Once inside, he had to suppress the impulse to dive for an adjoining door and make off down the corridor. He recognized the emotion. It was the same as that which had suddenly struck him in the little cottage in the jungle. Too many things were being pushed upon him too fast. He had to take time out, and take stock of his situation. But not now. Later.

The resolve relieved him. But still he stood, uncertain. That journey of minds and the lovemaking that was to follow it—Holroyd pondered that uneasily. The latter was, of course, unimportant. He had reached the age of thirty-three before coming to Gonwonlane, and if ever some super-being was to compile a list of young men of thirty or over who were white lilies, the name Holroyd would be conspicuously absent. No, the love-making part didn't matter, now that there was no question of the body and the woman not being one and the same. The disturbing thing was the journey of minds. What could it be?

Ineznia had been talking about having the rebels cut to pieces in the volcanic marshes and mountains of Nushirvan. And then she had said—What had she said? He couldn't remember clearly. He'd have to face it, whatever it was. There was no time to think about it now when so many other things were working in his favor. Satisfied, he placed the ring in a small transparent wall cabinet beside a large desk and walked slowly back into the room of the great windows.

CHAPTER XII

The Torn Page

THE GODDESS' BACK WAS TO HIM AS HOLROYD WALKED toward her across the thickly carpeted floor. He was able to study her with an objectivity that had not obtained while he was facing her. She was a small woman, not more than five feet in height. Her hair was her crowning glory. She wore it like a schoolgirl, and its cascading ripples shimmered with a soft, silken, golden luster. Sitting there, she looked like a child. The impression ended jarringly as Holroyd saw what she was holding in her lap: the great book containing the names of those whose executions she had desired such a short time before.

Holroyd smiled a pained smile, walked around, and sat down in his chair. The goddess looked up, her eyes thoughtful.

"I notice that you haven't signed this, Ineznio." Before Holroyd could speak, the goddess went on in a complaining voice, "You have never fully realized the importance of action against these people. Our whole younger generation is irreligious in the extreme, and self-assured, individualistic beyond bearance. A defeat, with their main leaders seemingly responsible—our propaganda will have to see to that—and most of those leaders killed—our military tactics will see to that—will frustrate them, leave them no psychological loophole. By skillful exploitation of the opportunity, we can stress that their contempt for prayer was responsible; and so send millions of the weaker-minded back to their prayer sticks. After that we may cease to worry. I have discovered that these rebellious outbursts never last more than a few generations. I leave the details to you."

Holroyd sat quiet, then he picked up his cup. The nir was still hot, and it was delicious. But a minute after his first sip, he couldn't have described how it tasted. In his mind's eye, he could see the picture she had so swiftly sketched—men, women, their souls hammered by catastrophe, going down listlessly to old age, to gloomy graves, without hope, without a single way to turn, while the golden, immortal goddess lived on, while the temples and their princes and emperors continued to exercise their iron control of a people so hopelessly enslaved that it was like . . . like *hell!*

Almost physically, ferociously, like a horse straining at a bit that was too tight, his mind champed on the determination that it should not be; it would not be.

The goddess was speaking again: "For the most part, as you can see, the executions are now unimportant. But—" her blue eyes measured him, "there is a page here, Ineznio, that I want you to sign. Every name on it is that of a person who is known to have committed murder. While they live, the law is insulted, my government put to scorn. You will sign it, will you not?"

She rushed on, "Ineznio, at times you infuriate me. You know as well as I that it has been my policy to permit you and my other—human—advisers to control the administration of government. I am interested only in the larger issues; this is one of them. You must sign this list."

Holroyd stared at her. The long though spasmodic harangue had given him an opportunity to plan his words. He said slowly, "Don't you think executions at this stage would arouse suspicions on the part of the very people whose minds you want to lull?"

Her answer startled him. There was a pen lying on the table. She snatched it, rippled furiously through the book, found the page she wanted and wrote rapidly in a blank space at the bottom of it. She finished with a flourish, grabbed the page and tore it out with a jerk. "There," she blazed, "this postpones all the executions for six months." She pushed the paper across the table and held out the pen. Her eyes glowed at him.

Without a word, Holroyd took the pen. He read the sentence she had written, then signed the single name, Ineznio, and silently handed the sheet back. Within six months he would have sat in the god chair. In six months he would be Ptath, or he would be dead. Besides, one page out of eighteen hundred. He couldn't have gotten more easily out of an impossible situation.

A finger touched his forehead. The goddess' voice caressed his ears:

"Come with me!"

CHAPTER XIII

Journey Of
Minds

BLURRED MOVEMENT! THAT WAS HOLROYD'S FIRST IMPRESsion. He shrank, expecting pain. But there was none. The blur lasted seconds, a sense of moving at enormous speed, then abruptly, the witch sight slowed. Instantly, he was gazing from a height at a vista of mountains. Mountains, mountains—and volcanoes!

As far as that eagle vision could penetrate the peaks towered to ever new heights, and the volcanoes poured their pall of smoke into the misty sky. There were hundreds of peaks, hundreds of volcanoes in sight, and vast valleys that hung thick with haze. Steam belched from dark fissures in the hide of the sullen, tortured land.

"Nushirvan," Holroyd thought—and felt his first pang of appalled doubt. "You couldn't send human beings into *that*."

But after a moment he knew better. Mountains could be taken by armies, volcanic land was never as bad as it looked; in fact the soil was usually so rich that vineyards and orchards prospered as nowhere else. Fascinated, he began an eye search for habitations. And found them. Houses crouched against hillsides, nestled in valleys dense with the haze of steam; and in the far distance where a valley ran almost straight toward the remote horizon, he could see the steeples and towers of a city. He thought instantly with a burning desire: Go there. Let us go there.

No, came the answer. It is impossible. I cannot cross the river of boiling mud.

Why not?

There was no reply to that; and Holroyd felt a brief blaze of impatience, and then—River of boiling mud! The name, the picture it evoked, caught his imagination. He peered down; and the strange thing then was that he should have missed it at all. Snakelike, the gray-dark mass undulated below. In and out along a great valley it wound. It averaged about a quarter of a mile in width, and a faint steam rose from its surface.

Armies coming up from the foothills of Gonwonlane would have to cross it. Once again the shocked wonder struck him like a blow: Could men be sent into such a hell? And again the knowledge came that they could and they must be. He could even visualize the type of built-in-advance pontoon bridge that could be used, one heavy enough to take monster tanks—or grimbs. There was not a soldier or officer on active service in World War II who had not crossed a hundred such bridges, frequently under fire.

On and on the journey of minds continued, following that broad river of mud in a westerly direction. Holroyd found himself estimating the speed of progress at about four hundred miles an hour. It was just fast enough to keep his interest at a high pitch, his mind working on the basis of his sharp observation, his whole being alert and eager. Once more he caught a tantalizing glimpse of a city half lost in the haze of distance. But that, too, lay beyond the river of boiling mud, uncrossable for some reason by this most perfect of all means of reconnaissance.

It was shortly after they passed the second city that the river turned sharply northward. Except for twistings and writhings that threaded around entire mountains, northward was its course thereafter. Holroyd began to feel puzzled. It was easy to understand the importance of the river where it faced Gonwonlane. But why follow the meandering course of a hot mud moat that seemed to encircle the solid core of Nushirvan? After an hour it was clear that that was exactly what they were doing. Gradually that remarkable canal twisted eastward, then after a long time—it seemed a long time now that his military interest had collapsed—it shifted south for yet more hours.

The sun, which had been high in the heavens, was clinging finally to the very edge of the western horizon, its rays casting long shadows over the strange, terrible mountain land of Nushirvan—when abruptly there was the blurry rush of speed that had begun the trip; and he was back in the palace.

The journey of minds, inexplicable because of the queer course it had followed, was over.

The room was much, much dimmer. Its great windows faced a still bright east, but twilight had obviously come early now that the sun was sinking in the west. Holroyd grew aware that he was slumped low in his chair; and that the goddess was regarding him from over the table with a faint, amused smile on her lips. Her eyes were serene. She looked at ease, comfortable, pleased with herself. Before Holroyd could speak, she said:

"I showed you the far side of Nushirvan, adjoining Accadistran, because I believe knowing about them will help you in planning your attack."

Holroyd couldn't quite see how. He parted his lips to say so, then shut them again. He who knew nothing about past discussions between Inezio and the goddess couldn't ask too many questions. Except that he *had* already asked one. And she had answered, unsatisfactorily, to be sure, but answered. He said:

"That river of boiling mud—why couldn't we cross it?"

The woman shook her head. The movement caused her hair to catch a flash of light. There was a fascinating glint of gold, like a fire stirred to life. Her voice came softly, out of the thickening gloom:

"There are some things, Inezio, that even you must not ask questions about, limitations to certain of my powers."

She was standing up. She came around the table and her arms were warm against his neck and cheek as she bent down. Her lips were cool at first, then demanding. The hard questions that still quivered in Holroyd's mind began to fade. "Later," he thought shakily, "I'll think this whole business through completely—"

Holroyd picked up the pen and wrote:

"The greatest power in Gonwonlane is the Goddess Ineznia. She brought Ptath here before he was due. How this was done was shown to me."

He stared at the paragraph with satisfaction. Just seeing it written down made him feel better. All day yesterday he had been rushed almost beyond his mental ability to keep up. Already the new morning had slowed the tempo of his life.

Here he was sitting at a writing desk alone, thinking over his problems in a leisurely fashion. The resulting general picture seemed distinctly clearer. L'onee had been sent against her will to bring him back to Gonwonlane, and she had done so. That was the beginning. By writing down everything in sequence, he ought to be able to fit in some of the pieces now missing, and draw decisive and important conclusions. Holroyd poised his pen, then wrote again:

"The second greatest power in Gonwonlane, but one greatly circumscribed, is L'onee. She frustrated the attempt of the Goddess Ineznia to snatch Ptath into the palace. How this frustration was accomplished was shown to me, and—" Holroyd stopped. He raised his pen and stared at the sentence. It was untrue. He *hadn't* been shown. He had been told. He whistled softly, then very swiftly, he began to write. In half an hour there was no more doubt. He scribbled his conclusions:

"The woman I thought L'onee is, of course, Ineznia. Accordingly, everything told to me by the temple princess, by Moora, the peasant girl, and by Marshal Nand's wife, is a distorted version, if not the exact reverse of the truth. The gaunt woman who tried to kill me, who gave me the ring, and who found speech so difficult, must be the real L'onee."

Holroyd leaned back and stared at the written words. The shock was mounting inside him, with wonder and a thousand questions flooding hard after, a totality that narrowed down to one surge of amazement: Why, *why* had she done everything as she had?

There could be only one answer to that. Ineznia would not have willingly given him a clue. She had done it all because she had to. Ptath in making his preparations for merging with the race hadn't been an absolute fool. He had left protectives. Holroyd enumerated them one by one on a sheet of paper.

"First: Evocation of a previous personality, presumably intelligent. The personality turned out to be Peter Holroyd." He paused, then added, "It seems hardly possible that Ptath could have desired such a confusing evocation. But call it the first protective.

"Second: The realm of darkness *had* to be shown. Third: A prayer stick in action. Fourth: A journey of minds, with its curious revelation that the goddess cannot penetrate Nushirvan beyond the river of boiling mud, which river completely surrounds the most thickly populated part of the outlaw state, like a moat. Fifth—''

Holroyd paused over the fifth. The how of it was more obscure. But there was no mistaking that Ineznia had regarded it as of vital importance. In the little cottage she had tried to get him to make love to the peasant girl, Moora. Holroyd frowned, but finally it seemed to him that he had it, not clearly, but understandable.

Sex was the great basic. In a world where a curious and terrible discovery had been made that, when men worshiped a woman in a certain rigid ceremonial—or woman a man—the woman became a goddess in actuality as well as in name, and the man a god—in such a world sex must have an intimate relation to the vastly greater organic force that was enslaving a nation of fifty-four billion souls. Man's terrible penchant to render homage to heroes, kings and non-existent gods had at last created divinity.

''The sixth protective,'' Holroyd wrote, ''must relate in some fashion to that page of people to be executed. She would never have insisted on my signature if it was not connected.''

He scowled pensively. The shock came suddenly, a lightning bolt of comprehension. Like a madman he leaped to his feet and raced into the great living room. The book was still there on the table. He snatched it and rippled to the L's. He found the torn segment. The last name immediately before the page that had been torn out was Lin'ra; the name at the top of the sheet immediately following the missing page was Lotibar.

There was no doubt at all. He had signed L'onee's death warrant. He stood grim and dismayed, assessing the extent of his ruin, and—what was more important—the hope that remained. Thank God, he thought, that his resistance had forced Ineznia to post date the sentences six months.

Slowly, realization came that there were other hopes. He hadn't sat in the god chair; and there must be something in connection with the river of boiling mud that was not yet in favor of Ineznia. And what about the attack on Nushirvan?

A knock on one of the doors stirred the developing blankness of his mind. The knocker was a woman guard, who said:

''Marshal Gara sends his compliments and wishes you to

be informed that the general staff is ready to leave for the Nushirvan front.''

Holroyd rattled off a speech he had prepared much earlier, one designed to get him to the starting point without the confusion of a search through a labyrinth of strange corridors. He said:

"Provide an escort for me to the place of departure. I shall be out in a moment."

He returned hastily to the writing room, tore to shreds the papers on which he had written his analysis, and then stood striving to shake thought into his head. Slowly, his mind grew colder, harder. He walked over to the cabinet beside the desk, took out the ring that had so briefly thwarted Ineznia's purpose, slipped it on—then strode into the living room, and picked up the great ledger with its list of rebels. The book should come in handy.

Deadlier grew his determination. The old Ptath couldn't have been such a fool as not to set traps for plotters. Accordingly, carry on until further reflections yielded a better plan. Attack Nushirvan; capture the so-called god-chair and, not necessarily sit in it, but even do that if nothing else suggested itself. Time was short, and caution never won a battle. Besides, what else was there to do?

CHAPTER XIV

Triumph of The Golden Goddess

THE BROOK BURBLED AND SWISHED. IN THE GRASS BESIDE it, L'onee sat combing her hair. She had taken off her clothes and the long, gaunt shape of the once dead body glinted brown and white in the sun. L'onee paused now, and leaned over the edge of the water to peer at her image. And smiled, not altogether displeased.

The body she had assumed, after a week of careful exposure to the warming rays of the sun, was beginning to show a life of its own. The hair, so lavishly brushed and combed, gleamed up at her with a dark luster. The green eyes had lost their fixed stare; the water reflected them as if two emeralds were there glowing in a soft light. The face—L'onee sighed. She had done her best with the face but it hadn't been enough. There it was, high cheekboned and long, and very plain.

She was still staring at it when, abruptly, she felt the approaching *presence*. She looked up. There was a flash of blue above the water ten feet away, a spinning shape of light and color and shade that came out of nothingness and took the living form of the Goddess Ineznia. The small, glistening, naked body seemed to poise for a moment, and then as it emerged all the way into materialization, it half fell, half leaped into the water.

Without haste, Ineznia waded out of the shallow pool. As L'onee stared curiously, Ineznia climbed onto the bank and seated herself in the grass two yards distant. Ineznia said scornfully, "You think you were very clever, don't you, giving him the ring with power."

L'onee shrugged. She half decided to answer, then changed her mind. Most of Ineznia's statements were rhetorical and not meant to evoke answers. She studied the serene face of the other. There was something in the unruffled expression that told of triumph. L'onee said softly:

"So he has signed my death warrant. But it can't be for right away. I would have known the moment you materialized. How long have I to live, Ineznia, darling?"

The serenity of the goddess' face broke before a ripple of exultant laughter. "You do not think that I will tell you that, do you?"

"Then," said L'onee tranquilly, "I shall carry on as if it's never."

It was a tiny victory to watch the frown of displeasure creep over Ineznia's delicate face. Then the rich voice snapped, "At least I can destroy your true body at will."

Sense of victory faded. L'onee gasped, "You mean, you haven't destroyed it yet?" She forced herself to stop. She was trembling, cold. Her true body! It was silly even to think about it now that she had so deliberately left it behind, but she couldn't help it. Believing it already destroyed, she had thought all the doubt resolved by the reality. But now everything that her body represented, the great beauty that had attracted and held mighty Ptath, the fact that it was a pole of god power—it was all still there for her to snatch if she could strike fast enough. She said huskily:

"You're even more clever than I believed, Ineznia. But not clever enough. I live or die with Ptath."

"It will be death—and soon," said the other coolly. "Five spells of the seven are canceled forever. His suspicion has now been aroused, I think, but it no longer matters. My net has snared him; and even spell number six is well on the way to dissolution. For it I have prepared a superb little plan that will nullify any independent thinking he may be doing. The new plan—really very old because it has been in my mind for a long time—will strike him down within a day or so. I thought," Ineznia finished placidly, "that I would put an end to any little hope you might have built up on the basis of your regained power and freedom."

L'onee sat weary. The tete-a-tete was going the way of most interviews in which Ineznia participated: the way of defeat. She let the silence gather, and after a little she felt better. Because her defeat was not as great as it seemed. For a week she had waited for Ineznia to come, deliberately keeping near water so that the coming would be easy. For a week she had wondered what was happening, and now she would find out. Curious, the vainglory in the golden goddess' character. Her own life as a captive would have been unbearable had it not been for Ineznia's frequent visits, Ineznia's eagerness to relate her exploits and her victories.

L'onee said quietly, "Frankly, I don't believe that he can organize a successful invasion of those volcanic mountains. After all, you tried seven times, and seven times the army failed to reach the chair of Ptath."

Ineznia made an impatient gesture. Her voice formed a pattern of sound against the quietness of that remote valley. At first L'onee listened to the sound, only vaguely aware of the sense. There was something in the other's tone, a note of accomplishment, as if this recital was about an event that had already had its culmination, about a triumph already scored.

In one or two days, Ineznia had said, her plan would work out. The truth must be, one or two days *ago*. Or perhaps it was happening now, this hour, while she sat talking. What was she saying?

". . . He gave a lecture on the second day of his arrival at the front to ten thousand marshals and their wives. I was one of the wives. Everything he said coincided with my own recent thinking on military strategy, the importance of increasing out of all present proportion the number of freight-carrying screers and grimbs. It was interesting, particularly because—"

Ineznia paused. She smiled. Then she said in a sugary voice:

"Only you, my darling L'onee, know about *that*. And your tongue is sealed, is it not, sweet? But you will know what I mean when I tell you that the key word is Accadistran."

L'onee said in a steely rage, "You devil! You incredible murderess!"

Elfin laughter shimmering in a tonal harmony cut across her words. The laughter ended in the abrupt fashion that left no doubt at all of the humorlessness of the mind and soul behind it. Ineznia said coldly:

"How sentimental we are. What can it possibly matter if a human being dies a few years before his time."

She lay back on the grass with an air of having time to spend. Her perfect body gleamed white in the blaze of the morning sun. But her eyes were like blue marble as she stared along the brook and the valley, where it spread toward the northern hills. She seemed lost in contemplation of L'onee's screer which stood like some great fisher bird, its long-beaked head darting again and again into the stream, emerging each time with a white-bellied fish.

It seemed to L'onee that she could almost read the thoughts behind Ineznia's stare. But it was obvious, finally, that the golden goddess knew better than to attempt to break an established animal control. Ineznia sighed and said:

"Too bad Ptath delivered his lecture so soon instead of waiting till after he had appointed rebel officers to high commands. I feel sure his earnest manner, his immense confidence, and the substance of his words would have dissipated even their suspicion. I must admit I was surprised myself at the bold manner in which he has taken command of such a vast army." She looked up thoughtfully, said, "I doubt if the man Holroyd realizes that only a demi-Ptath could have grasped such power as he has already taken. Of course, it doesn't matter now that the rebels have fallen for a little trick of mine."

She paused, smiling with such glee that L'onee stared at her. In spite of her own previous analysis that there was a triumph here already completed, or in the process of completion, L'onee had the blank sense of an exultation out of place.

"Trick?" she echoed.

Ineznia's rich voice, aglow now, went on, "Yesterday he led rebel officers and artists, mounted on screers, on an aerial reconnaissance. This morning he has taken another group, mounted on grimbs, to survey the same area on the basis of the sketches drawn yesterday."

"But I don't see—" L'onee began emptily.

"You will, my dear," the goddess spoke caressingly, "when I tell you that two days ago I allowed to fall into the hands of the rebel General—now Marshal—Maarik, a document purporting to be from Ineznio to me, in which the entire invasion was shown to be a trick designed to destroy the rebels."

She stood up lazily, her hair flashing fire-gold in the sun from the movement. "The rebels," she said, "are taking action on that this morning. As a result, *my* design—to break the sixth spell—will be accomplished today. By tonight the god chair will be in my control.''

Her smile shone at L'onee. ''The reason I acted with such dispatch, you will be happy to know, is because your escape, with the power I had to give you, provided an unexpected obstacle with which I am taking no chances. Good-bye, darling.'' She stepped into the water—and vanished.

For a long moment L'onee stared bitterly at the spot where Ineznia had disappeared. So the one week she had allowed herself, the week that would give this half-dead body time to come further into life—that week had proved too long. She began slowly to dress. It was difficult to know what she should have done. She had counted on the attack on Nushirvan requiring time to mount. Now, her own dim plan, with its emphasis on helping Ptath to learn the truth of what he faced—that limited plan must be speeded up, adjusted somehow to the new situation.

Her immediate objective was obvious. She must find Ptath. Wherever he was, she must seek him out. His headquarters would be in the central hills, opposite the city Three of Nushirvan. Somewhere in that enormous spread of valleys and ever steeper hills, with its confusing totality of men and beasts, would be Ptath—in trouble. She finished buckling her sandals, forced the screer to come to her, and a minute later was flying into the northwest.

CHAPTER XV

The River Of
Boiling Mud

"OUTLAWS!" HOLROYD HEARD SOMEONE SAY.

"Eh?" He spoke sharply. He stiffened slowly in his saddle on the back of the grimb. Startled, he stared at the long line of riders coming across the green valley. His eyes narrowed. Outlaws here *behind* the army encampments, after all the precautions he had taken. Beside him a man's voice said softly:

"About five hundred. That's two to one. How does it feel, great lord Ineznio, to be facing peril yourself instead of being so cool and self-possessed about the depredations of the Nushirvan outlaws that you agreed to a counterfeit invasion?"

Holroyd sent the speaker a shocked look. The man was small, dressed in the uniform of a colonel, but there was an insolence in his manner, an air of assured command, that marked him as a person far more important in some other organization. Holroyd sighed. He had been so set on his own plans that the possibility of suspicion on the part of the people whose cause he was particularly upholding had not seriously entered his mind. So the rebels had somehow found out about the goddess' original seeming intention to make a pretended attack. With grim humor they had made an arrangement with the outlaws to capture the man they thought was Prince Ineznio. Sitting there, his dismay must have surged into his face, because the thick-cheeked young colonel laughed loudly, then said in a steely voice:

"You've been here a week, and you haven't fooled anybody with your sudden appointing to command positions of men who have long favored an attack on Nushirvan. The important thing about that trick is that they now *have* the commands. The general orders are known to all high officers. To fool those not in on our plan, we have forged some beautiful letters stating that you are going on a recruiting tour. The attack *will* take place, but it won't be any half-measure. One month from today the army moves.''

The first shock was over. Holroyd sat quiet, grimmer now. He sent a quick glance at the approaching line of outlaws. They seemed to be in no hurry, sure of their prey. They were still half a mile away. The gap of distance brought no comfort. The god Ptath, with his present strength, could not handle this situation.

And yet he must not be captured. Didn't these fools realize that the Gonwonlanian army wasn't ready for any attack on such a mountain fortress as Nushirvan? There must be three, four, five months of regrouping, at least. And there must be night and day accumulation of supplies. On top of that it was vital that the screer and grimb transport service be organized to include at least two out of every three birds and beasts on the entire vast continent. Blitz and a flexible transport system was the answer to the appalling mountains, the glaring volcanoes, the bubbling black quicksands that formed the enormous, uneasy isthmus of Nushirvan. Curt laughter welled up inside him. Who among that great concourse of officers would know what to do with a hundred million animals and birds?

Beside Holroyd, the colonel said, "It's foolish even to think of resisting. Look behind you. There's five hundred more. You can't escape this ambush.''

Holroyd did not turn. Out of the corner of his eye he had seen a movement on the lip of the steep hill that formed the right flank of this green gem of a valley. Riders! They charged over the rim and raced down the rough slopes. It was recklessly, superbly done. A quick glance over his left shoulder showed that the other flank of the valley was disgorging riders from a narrow ravine. The ring was complete, with no military brilliance involved, simply a dependence on over-whelming force.

Unhurriedly, now that it was clear that the incidence of the outlaws' presence must run its course, Holroyd reexamined his personal position. And realized that two hopes existed. He urged his grimb forward toward a slender man who sat tall on his mount at the head of the line of grimbs. The officer saw him coming and watched his approach with a grave smile that actually ended the first hope then and there. But Holroyd did not pause. He rode up; he said curtly:

"Marshal Uubrig, you will order the men to scatter in all directions with the purpose of confusing the enemy and the possibility that some will escape."

He saw that the other was looking at him curiously. "Will I, sir?" the officer drawled finally. He went on in a gentle voice, "I think it would be rather difficult to persuade the men. It's a special group, you know. Everyone here has lost sister or brother, mother or father to the outlaws. They realize that the Nushirvan are untrustworthy. They are convinced they are sacrificing themselves, but believe that your capture makes it worthwhile. Do you think, my great Prince Ineznio," Marshal Uubrig finished ironically, "that men of such mind would rush to obey my orders if I should suddenly command them as you directed?"

Holroyd was silent. He had neglected to consider the outlaws. Almost blankly, he went over in his mind his past attitude toward Nushirvan. He hadn't really thought of it from their point of view. They had been blurs, much like the Germans after his first emotional hatred of their collective actions yielded to the hard, bitter reality of fighting.

Attack Nushirvan, L'onee had said; and the appalling trickery of the goddess, her abnormal attempts to avoid such an attack, had intensified his own convictions that the invasion must be launched. Now, of course, it seemed that her actions had been merely a trick to get him to make the attack.

He saw that the nearest of the riders was only two or three hundred yards away. He'd have to hurry and find someone who would co-operate in carrying out his second hope. He whirled his mount, parted his lips to yell his request, and then hesitated. It was one thing to remember what Ptath had gone through physically; it was another thing entirely to force himself deliberately to do the same thing.

The riders were a hundred yards away. "Is there any man here," Holroyd shouted, "who will put an arrow through my heart?"

No one answered. No one moved. The brilliantly garbed officers glanced at each other, and then glanced uneasily at the charging outlaws.

"You see"—it was the colonel, who came up beside

him—"we promised to deliver you alive. Our only hope that they will let us go is that we do deliver you—alive!"

Holroyd had no sense of desperation now. He felt cool, collected, determined. He *had* to escape this ridiculous kidnapping. Out there at headquarters he had free will, a chance to think things over. Here, once more, was that deadly pressure of too much happening too swiftly, which had already brought him to the verge of ruin.

He saw that the colonel carried one of those beautifully slender hardwood, stone-tipped lances that officers sported. Before the man was even aware of his intention, Holroyd had urged his grimb over. There was the briefest fight over the possession of the weapon. The officer's eyes widened as the lance was torn from his grip as if he were a small child. Holroyd twisted away triumphantly. He whipped the spear around, and, because there wasn't an instant to waste, plunged the weapon into his left breast, hard and deep. He was only vaguely aware of the churning arrival of more than fifteen hundred outlaws.

The pain was hideous for a moment. Then the agony faded. Holroyd could still feel the pressing of the lance against his body where it had entered. It was an unpleasantly heavy weight that he would have to get rid of as soon as he possibly could. He let himself slump slowly backward onto the broad, smooth back of the beast he rode, taking care to keep his feet in the leather stirrups. Nearby somebody bellowed in a guttural rage but the language was Gonwonlanian.

"So this is the way you deliver the body. The Nushir will make somebody pay for this. Round them all up, the dirty traitors."

The colonel's voice protested. "It was not our fault. You saw yourself how he grabbed my lance and killed himself. Who'd ever expect pleasure-loving Ineznio to do that?"

Holroyd felt a bleak sympathy for the man. These rebels were right, basically. No group ever had been braver, defying an unkillable woman and a religio-slave set-up of temple potentates more powerful than anything that had ever existed anywhere. And each man here had taken his part in this dangerous rendezvous with the outlaws, knowing that he might never return.

"Dead or not, I've got to deliver his body!" the outlaw

leader roared. "Now, get a move on, all of you. We can't waste time here."

There was a heavy stamping of claw-armored paws; and then movement that became a flowing run. After ten minutes, Holroyd thought bitterly: They could at least have removed the lance from his body. The weapon began to worry him. It seemed incredible that he could go on all day with such a solid shaft pushed squarely into his breast. The organic structure of the Ptath body must be *radical*.

Holroyd slitted his eyes and lay for a moment blinking at a sun that was still far from mid-heaven. In flinging himself backward as he had, he had put himself into an awkward position. He let his head roll sideways, but there was still more sky than ground in his range of vision.

Far away he saw a big screer, with a single rider, flapping northward. Holroyd thought, "If only the fool on the bird's back would realize what was happening. There was still time to send a warning that would cut off this venturesome crew of outlaws from the Nushirvan border." But as he watched gloomily, the bird vanished into the mists over a hill.

Conscious again of the lance, Holroyd allowed himself to tilt forward, slowly, as a dead man might under the capricious pressure of movement. It took the most careful manipulation but finally he succeeded in establishing a solid base for the shaft end of the lance at the lower end of the grimb's neck. He began to press forward. There was a flash of pain as the lance pierced out of his back. But he clamped his teeth and pushed harder. It took time to push it through. There were new bases to be established for bracing the shortening shaft. Finally, however, he lay flat forward on the back of the grimb and he could feel the unsteady pressure of the lance as it wavered above him like a flagless flagpole in a rushing wind.

From the corner of his eyes, Holroyd studied his situation. There was an outlaw riding on either side of him, the one on the left almost directly opposite. If he could roll over—He did. Instantly, a bass voice grunted in pain, then cursed.

"Oh, shut up!" a nearby voice commanded. "Tear that lance out of him. It's unbalancing the corpse. I noticed it was working its way through."

The sense of weight ended. Holroyd lay quiet. He had a

heady conviction of victory. "Tonight," he thought savagely, "tonight under cover of darkness and volcanic mists, who would watch a dead body?" There was a yell from the bass voice, then shouted words:

"Hey, look, chief! There's no blood on this spear. Something's wrong."

There was indeed. In a minute Holroyd's grimb halted. Rough hands caught him, pulled him to the ground and fumbled over him. Then the leader's voice, hard with satisfaction, said:

"No wounds. I thought it funny the goddess' lover should be so mortal. Better snap out of it, Prince Ineznio."

Without a word, Holroyd climbed to his feet and mounted his grimb. Almost to a man the outlaws were big, tall men. Many were bearded or mustached. From such a rough-and-ready crew, Holroyd expected ridiculing laughter. But there was none. Men looked at him and when he returned their stare they wouldn't face it, but glanced away hastily. The rebels acted the same way, which was worrying. Because it was important that he make friends with somebody. The general reaction seemed unnatural until he tried to picture what they had seen: a man with a lance through his heart rising unharmed, and active.

On and on pounded the long columns, winding through ever wilder foothills. Noon brought no pause. A small wooden basket of food was handed to Holroyd by one of the outlaws, but the other prisoners, Holroyd noted, received nothing.

He examined his basket with interest. It contained three types of fruit, one of which he had not seen before. It was round and about three inches in diameter. It had a thick, soft, red skin that peeled like a banana. The fruit tasted like a grape. The parcel contained no bread, or other foods, just the fruit.

The seesaw of movement had brought a rebel officer opposite him. To him, Holroyd said:

"If you will promise to eat what I have here, you can have it. In a crisis I can do without food for"—he paused, smiled with grim memory; finished—"for seven hundred years."

The officer said curtly, "Go to Accadistran!"

The long afternoon waned, and still Holroyd did not eat the fruit. Food was food, more precious to a hungry man than ideals. But the partly peeled grape was turning a rusty color when once more his own beast and that of the other officer—General Seyteil; Holroyd recalled the name vaguely—matched strides.

"General," Holroyd said earnestly, "have you any idea how far we are from the river of boiling mud?"

The officer, a lean, hawk-nosed man of forty, hesitated, then shrugged.

"We should reach it well before dark," he said. "There are about a dozen bridge approaches to the city Three, which lies about eight kanbs beyond the river."

Holroyd nodded, worried. He mustn't cross that river. Ineznia's inability to cross even mentally must mean something. He'd have to think it over, and quickly. He studied the profile of the rebel officer, but there was a granite quality there that promised nothing, in spite of the fact that the man had already answered one of his questions. The other's resistance would take time and effort to overcome; and time was one of the things that was lacking.

Moodily, Holroyd stared at the hills. Higher they were now than when the journey had started. And in the near distance ahead still others spired and turreted, domed and minareted to ever new heights, and already some shed smoke into a sky that was growing ever hazier. He could almost feel the world of mist that was Nushirvan closing, closing around him. He turned again to the officer.

"This food," he said urgently above the pounding of heavy paws, "I swear it is not my intention to eat it. If you don't want it, pass it on to somebody who doesn't know it comes from me. Food knows nothing of hate or ideology."

The man took the basket this time, ate the huge grape, and handed the container to another rebel. Holroyd did not bother to trace the food further. He said:

"Suppose I were to swear that I came to the Nushirvan front to fight and conquer, would that make any difference in the attitude of yourself and the others?"

"None at all," was the reply. "Prince Ineznio is a puppet of the goddess. We know exactly what she is."

"Suppose," said Holroyd grimly, "I told you I was not Ineznio? That I was—Ptath."

The officer turned and stared at him with appraising eyes. Finally, he laughed.

"That's clever. There's only one thing wrong. No one can convince us that such a person as Ptath ever existed." He broke off. "I seem to have underestimated our speed. There's the river of boiling mud just ahead. We should be in the city Three by evening."

It was as swift as that. Approaching the stone bridge that spanned the river of mud, the grimbs broke step. Holroyd had a brief glimpse of bubbling mud and there was a sense of heat, countless flashes of steam. In half an hour they were all across. Deeper and deeper into the land of Nushirvan they raced.

CHAPTER XVI

The City Three

AS THE BRIDGE RECEDED BEHIND THE LONG CARAVAN, HOLROYD grew conscious of exhilaration—like a man, he thought grimly, on his way to the execution chamber. But the dark comparison wouldn't stay in his mind. It didn't fit. He had a sense of being in the midst of great events, an immense, wondering conviction. Could mortal man desire more than this: to be two hundred million years in the future, a demigod in a fantastic land?

Ptath! Mighty Ptath! If only he could snatch the great power that was here, he'd crush the damnable temple civilization. The thought flagged. He grew aware of the intensity of his feelings, an intensity that had not existed before the crossing of the bridge. He sat very still on the broad back of the grimb, letting his mind relax, his whole being grow quiet. He waited, watching for some inward sign that would indicate new and terrible personal strength. But there was only the flowing movements of the monster he rode.

Holroyd shook himself in sudden fury. Damn it, there must be a difference. He *felt* different, more alert, eager rather than depressed. His gaze fell on the ring that had so startled Ineznia. Memory came of the fairy tales of his childhood. With a wry smile he caught the ring, twisted it three times, said:

"By this ring I demand to be transported instantly to my headquarters in Gonwonlane."

His smile deepened as the seconds fled and nothing happened. He tried again, his anger forgotten. But there was still nothing. He had known, of course. God-power was not just hocus-pocus. It grew out of one of the deepest, most sustained of human emotional complexes. Old, old was that impulse, that mass urge to devotion and obedience. And, somewhere, long ago, a king named Ptath had been lifted up to the status of genuine godhood that had been potential from the first moment that a primitive vassal prostrated himself abjectly at the broad, naked feet of the first chieftain-priest.

And of course, once so cataclysmic a force was discovered, other men of steel would learn about it, recognize its nondivine origin, and strive with unutterable ambition to participate in the glory that issued naturally to the fortunate controller. Once discovered, the great power could only be transferred; it could never be destroyed. Always a new god ruler would replace the fallen one. Such force would never again vanish from the affairs of men. Even Ptath had believed that he was assuring his ultimate reassumption of the shining mantle, ere he laid it aside to sink into his incomprehensible merging with the race.

But why had Ptath done such a foolish thing in the first place? The answer to that could easily have a bearing on events now proceeding. But no answer came to Holroyd. His mind might as well have remained blank. The questions raged through him and all that mattered in the end was the tireless flowing run of the grimb. On and on raced the powerful convoy of prisoners and captors, pushing higher and higher into the ever higher foothills.

Holroyd saw his first castle. It was a dark stone structure that squatted like an enormous cone-hatted witch in the center of a spread of houses on top of a fortified hill. The sight brought a thrill, then a savage eagerness, and knowledge of the military tactics that must be used against such a formidable obstacle in a world that lacked siege artillery. Screer-mounted troops flung down in masses that would saturate the defenses of each fort in turn. Carried out with sufficient blitz violence, casualties should be extremely light. Such forces could safely attack three days ahead of the ground forces and paralyze the communications of the enemy. Apparently, in the seven attacks mentioned by the history books, nothing like that had ever been tried. Thank God, he had outlined the plan to some high marshals.

The shadows in the valleys began to lengthen. The sun glowed blood-red as it sank toward a smoking volcano in the western hills. There were carts now, pulled by dottles, on a smaller side road, a steady stream of them coming from behind a hill that loomed ahead. They turned off into scores of branching roads that led toward forts and buildings that crowned every hilltop. The head of the long column started to round the hill. Suddenly, a great shout echoed from them. The cry was taken up, and swept down the line in a gathering crescendo:

"The Nushir! The Nushir's standard flies from the central fort. The Nushir has come in person to interview the Prince Ineznio—"

A minute later, Holroyd's own grimb rounded the hill; and he saw the city Three spread before and above them. What the Nushirvan called the great collection of buildings was a mystery that had been lost in the ages. There was a vague story—he had been told by an officer a few days before—that its name was Yit or Yip or Yik. But on all the Gonwonlane military maps it was known simply as Three. Which meant that only two other outlaw cities were closer to the border. And one of these was far to the west, the other equally far to the east.

Three stood on an enormous plateau and climbed the hills to the rear; and in the dusk it was like a city out of the legends of Am, dark, curiously unwholesome, a strange nebulous dream out of antiquity. The wind which brought the subdued rumble of the city to Holroyd wafted also odd odors, a not unpleasant intermingling of kitchen smells with the scent of grimb stables and screer aeries. All-pervading was that perfume; and as the long line of riders padded swiftly along the dimming streets it became the air they breathed, thick, normal, almost rich and—Holroyd smiled grimly— probably quite healthy.

"Prince," said the voice of General Seyteil.

Holroyd turned. Before he could verbally acknowledge the call, the hawk-nosed officer went on swiftly:

"I've been thinking of what you said back there!" The general made a movement with his head. "If you're Ptath, why haven't you asserted your power?"

Holroyd made no immediate answer. He had forgotten completely his attempt to win this man over. Forgotten it the instant the river of boiling mud was crossed, and his purpose of securing help to prevent a crossing was frustrated by the event. His attention concentrated slowly on the general. Realizing that his delay in answering might look like stalling for time, he began to explain his situation to the officer. The man cut him off in a violent astonishment:

"You mean when you crossed that moat of mud you smashed a spell that had kept the goddess out of Nushirvan?"

"I don't understand how it worked," Holroyd said. "I've been trying to think of it as something planted in her mind, which she couldn't nullify in spite of all the power she has accumulated."

It was darker now, harder to see the other man. The streets were lighted by dull light sticks that sent a dim glow through the mist of darkness and fog that was thickening over the city. A coolness came down from the hills, making it comfortable after the blazing heat of the day, but the intensity of the night that was falling only emphasized how near was the end of the journey and the parting of the ways that would come with it. Holroyd spoke hurriedly:

"General, what made you speak to me in the first place?"

There was no answer, and after a moment Holroyd shrugged. He rode on in silence for a while, grim, then he said:

"I presume most of you are sent on to Accadistran. What does the Zard do with kidnaped people?"

This time there was satiric laughter out of the darkness. Then the general said:

"The report is the Zard wants colonists. But since no prisoners have ever escaped from such a colony, we suspect the worst. There are incredible stories— As for why I spoke to you, it seemed to me your claim to be Ptath might be of benefit to us whether or not you actually are Ptath. Your story about the rebel Tar at the temple Linn could be verified, you know."

The officer finished in a disconnected fashion, "As I say, I was thinking of that, and then I remembered our position. And realized that we're subject to"—he laughed softly—"change without notice. Oh! We're slowing."

It was so. Deceleration was as smooth and jerkless as had been the entire journey. The great beasts cut their pace naturally, by the simple process of ceasing their forward pressure. Momentum carried them on with an easy, graceful motion. They poured between two lighted posterns; and for a long moment after they had come to a stop it was hard to realize that dynamic action had merged so naturally into utter passivity.

Men surrounded Holroyd. "This way, Prince Ineznio. You are to be taken at once to the noble Nushir."

He was led along a great marble corridor that opened into a vast room at the far end of which sat a man and two women.

CHAPTER XVII

The Nushir Of Nushirvan

THE NUSHIR OF NUSHIRVAN WAS A BIG, PLUMP, BLUE-EYED young man. The throne chairs of his wives were set partly behind his large one, but both were to his right.

As Holroyd stepped into the room, the two women automatically leaned toward each other, whispered simultaneously and then nodded in unison. One was slender and dark, one was plump and fair, and their action was so much as if they had thought the same thought, and spoke it, all in a spirit of perfect agreement, that Holroyd's attention was caught to them. It cost him a distinct effort to disengage his mind and concentrate on the fact that the Nushir was speaking. He was dimly aware that the guards had withdrawn beyond closed doors.

The plump man said in a soft voice, "You are truly Ineznio?"

There was obscene eagerness in the creature. He leaned forward. His eyes glistened with an off-color, blue avidity that made Holroyd wary as he nodded his reply. There was no doubt at all that the hereditary outlaw chieftain had had a purpose in making a deal with the rebels for Ineznio's capture. Holroyd waited tensely as the man said:

"And you are in charge of the attack that is being mounted against my country?"

Comprehension struck along every nerve of Holroyd's body. He stared at his too plump interrogator with narrowed eyes, fascinated by the personal potentialities of the situation. If he handled this right, he could be free in ten minutes. He stood letting the picture, the full weight of the idea sink in. And every quiver of the man's palpitating anxiety was suddenly understandable and it fitted.

The dull-blue eyes shone with an unlovely ardor, the big,

111

plump hands opened and closed as if they were grasping, reaching, toward an intensely desired object. The thick lips hung agape, and the soft, heavy nose dilated. The entire physical appearance of the ruler showed the truth. The Nushir of Nushirvan had learned that he was about to be attacked. And, in spite of the failure of past invasions, he was alarmed by this new threat. Holroyd drew a deep breath, said, "If your defensive precautions are at all normal, you won't have to worry."

"What do you mean?"

"The attack," said Holroyd coolly, "is being made to satisfy dissonant elements. There is no intention of forcing it to a conclusion. By having me captured, you have played into the hands of the very people who want to destroy you."

"He's lying." It was the dark-haired woman, her voice thin and harsh. She tugged at the fat arm of her master. "He hesitated too long before answering, and besides there is something in his manner. Put him to the torture instantly. We must know."

"Ah," said Holroyd, "I see the government in Nushirvan is the same as in Gonwonlane."

The odd blue eyes studied him bleakly. There was uncertainty in them and curiousity. Finally, the Nushir said:

"Explain that."

"Both are run by women," said Holroyd coolly; and the two women gasped. In their automatic fashion they bent toward each other but each must have drawn a blank response for they straightened and sat looking baffled.

The Nushir merely sat sluggish, more impassive, but he wiggled his head with the faintest impatience as the dark woman tugged again at his arm. She did not seem to be aware of her master's mood, for she spoke, half to him, half, defiantly, to Holroyd:

"There is only one ruler in all Nushirvan. But we are his wives. We have his interests at heart. We shine only as a reflection of his glory. When we advise him it is as instruments of his body. In this case we are the tools who sensed your lie. Therefore we advise torture—immediately."

She almost snapped the last word and then sat glaring at Holroyd, who whistled ruefully under his breath. His attempt to drive a wedge between husband and wives was backfiring badly. The hard wonder came: just what could torture that included, for instance, amputation, do to a body such as his? The chilling speculation ended as he saw the expression that was changing—transforming—the face of the blond wife.

She had seemed at first glance nondescriptly good-looking; her position as second from the Nushir's chair placed her as a lesser wife. She grew different. She straightened physically, and the move seemed mental as well. Her eyes glowed with life; color surged into her cheeks. She sat very still for an instant, as if in deep thought, then she said in a ringing voice:

"Speak for yourself, Niyi. If the prince is speaking the truth—and what we know of Gonwonlane supports his statements—then he is our ally, not our enemy; and a conference under more gracious circumstances, after breakfast tomorrow morning, is in order. I suggest that our guest be furnished with a woman for the night and assigned an apartment."

There was silence. Twice, Niyi, the dark, parted her lips to speak; twice she turned with clenched fist toward the blond woman, but each time her astonishment seemed to override both her voice and her will to action. She glanced finally at her lord and waited.

Thoughtfully, the Nushir sat stroking his smooth, fat chin. But at last he began to nod his head. He said:

"It shall be so, for such is the conclusion I also have drawn. In view of the high rank of our guest he may choose one of my two wives here present. In the morning we shall talk and then, if everything is satisfactory, a screer escort shall return the Lord Ineznio to his own lines." He paused, ended, "Which of my two wives, great prince?"

Refusal didn't even enter into the matter. To do so would be to give a mortal insult. And the choice required scarcely a thought, so obvious it was. Holroyd said gravely:

"I select her who has been called Niyi, and thank you for thus honoring me, great Nushir. You shall not regret it."

He was thinking: What a fool he'd be to leave the dark hostile woman alone with her husband for a night of unopposed propaganda. The Nushir was speaking:

"I would have thought," he said in an interested tone, "that, like the others who have been thus honored, you would have chosen blond Calya." He shrugged, smiled, "It will be an interesting experience for you, Niyi."

He tugged at a silken cord that hung down from the ceiling. Instantly, attendants swarmed into the room. Within ten minutes, Holroyd was alone with his wife-for-a-night.

There was a great, ornamental window at the far end of the main room. With scarcely a glance at the dark woman, Holroyd walked toward it and stared out. The city Three spread below him. Its dimly glowing street light stick gave an overall effect of an old European city in partial blackout.

The sense of exhilaration that had come after the crossing of the bridge was stronger now. In spite of everything, tendrils of satisfaction coiled through his mind. It was true that he had suffered a defeat in having to cross the river of boiling mud, but he had also won his freedom to return to Gonwonlane. Just what the balance was between the defeat and the victory he, who knew so little, could not hope to judge. It was probably adverse, but at least being free would give him a chance to think things over and prepare for the next onslaught. Right here and now he must draw a line and say: No further. Action henceforth *must* be based on information and the profoundest consideration.

Holroyd laughed curtly. One man in a world that he knew almost nothing about, with great decisions to make, couldn't possibly learn anything of importance in time. Still it felt better to be free!

He drew his mind from speculation and remembered Niyi. He would take her, naturally, in the sense that she had been offered. Any dereliction on his part would probably be reported, and would be considered bad manners—not to be risked. He turned from the window and stared in astonishment. The dark woman was standing with one ear pressed against the corridor door, listening intently. She rolled her eyes and looked at Holroyd, and then—amazing action—put a finger on her lips in the ancient admonition. Finally, with a graceful flowing movement, she came gliding over.

"We shall have to act swiftly," she hissed. "You made things very difficult by selecting Niyi instead of Calya, whose body I entered just before she spoke in your favor. Now, I have had to switch to this one; and the blond woman will be remembering that she was possessed, not clearly, and that will give us a little time, but enough to alarm her eventually into speech."

She paused; and Holroyd said violently, "What the—" He stopped and stood as still as stone, his eyes like two slits. So he was being rushed once more!

"Who are you?" he said harshly.

The woman whispered, "I am she who climbed the great cliff, who tried to kill you, and who gave you the ring of Ptath. Search back in your mind: Did you tell anyone that you saw me? If not, then you must *know* that I am not Ineznia."

She rushed on, unheeding of his efforts to speak:

"We dare not delay, I swear it. At this very moment Ineznia is in the Nushir's central palace striving desperately to destroy the god chair of Ptath. The chair is the last of the—"

Her voice grew thick, as if her tongue was suddenly too big for her mouth. She swallowed hard, tried again, then gave up the sentence that had caused the painful stoppage. She finished urgently:

"We must go there without delay. An hour, *even* a minute might be too late. Ptath, I realize only too clearly how often you have been fooled. But it cannot be helped. You must take one more chance—now!"

The odd thing was that Holroyd's resolve, which had seemed so firm, so deep-rooted, should yield before one verbal onslaught. But what she had said was true. He hadn't told anyone about the gaunt woman; and Ineznia's very dismay at the sight of the ring was like a stamp of approval now on her who had given it to him. Ineznia didn't know, *didn't* know how this woman had come to him, even though she had probably guessed that she had come. Therefore, this was the aeon-imprisoned L'onee; and if L'onee was now telling him that he had no time to lose, then he hadn't.

Now that he thought of it, Ineznia's action in having him kidnaped showed a contemptuous disregard of the suspicion it might arouse. She hadn't been like that in her earlier attitude. It must mean that the culmination of her plans was in sight. The protective edifice that Ptath had built long ago was crashing. The maddest thing was that, thinking thus, he was still standing here. But he couldn't help it. The weight of his hesitation, and the reason behind it, was too important to ignore. He had been told that he must sit in the god chair of Ptath, and that by so doing he would regain the old, tremendous god power of Ptath.

It sounded ludicrous, a child's game. But *both* Ineznia and L'onee had told him that it was so. Why had Ineznia imparted to him one great truth among so many lesser lies? Why had she told him about the chair at all? She must have told him for the same reason that had made it necessary for her to reveal in some way, by action or word, the other protectives now canceled. And besides, telling him had been psychologically correct. It had focused his mind on that distant goal, while she accomplished every one of her secondary purposes. But now, she was on the last lap. And action on the most desperate scale was imperative.

He saw that—L'onee—was watching him with wide, tragic eyes. He felt briefly appreciation that she had not interrupted his necessary thought, then hurriedly he said:

"How can we leave here?"

"If you will follow me as if we were going for a walk," she answered. "The warm flying clothes are in a chamber next to the screer aeries—Niyi is the chief wife. As Niyi I can command a screer escort at any time of the day or night without questions. Come!"

Holroyd raced beside her for the door, then, "Wait!" he said. "There's a General Seyteil among the prisoners. Is there some way that he could be provided with a screer and allowed to escape? I have an idea he could be doing valuable work in Gonwonlane while—"

L'onee cut him off. "It's impossible. Such an action would be out of character. Besides, we haven't time for *anything!* Hurry!"

In fifteen minutes the flight was begun.

CHAPTER XVIII

Land Of The
Volcanoes

IT GREW VERY COLD. YET STILL HIGHER LOOMED THE REACH-
ing mountains ahead, dark and bleak and savage under the
strange, near stars. But all was not bleakness. In that freezing
world volcanic fires leaped and flared from a thousand craters,
making the night hideous and terrible with red flame and
red-black smoke. Each cone of fire seemed to hold itself
aloof, and somehow the night around was darker, the
nonvolcanic mountains colder and more awesome. The screers
avoided the air above the spitting craters, stayed up and out
where the cold was unalloyed, like sheeted ice.

Distinctly, Holroyd felt the great, struggling bird beast, on
which L'onee and he were mounted, grow sluggish and weary.
Twice, with a sharp anxiety, he saw it and the others of that
concourse scramble desperately in their barely successful effort to breast upjutting knobs of mountain.

When the downward journey began he had no clear
knowledge. Perhaps it was when his mind began with instinct
of its own to reach ahead and strive to visualize what the end
of the journey would bring. In any event, suddenly the birds
were flying easier, faster; and the air grew perceptibly warmer.
A city sprinkled its lights from below. Then another, and
another. Even the ground in between the larger masses of
lights was not dark finally, but shot with countless streaky
patches of dull-white glow points. The first cities nestled in
valleys between enormous peaks, but swiftly that jagged
barrier yielded to foothills, then to a flatter land. The air grew
balmy and the cities unending. The next one was always in
sight before the previous one so much as grew dim.

It was about an hour and a half after they left the foothills
that L'onee turned in her saddle and shouted downwind at
Holroyd:

"Khotahay, the capital!"

The way she spoke the name it had an exotic, a heart-quickening music in its pronunciation. But in the night the city looked like all the others except that it was bigger, and it spread to a range of hills in the north, and silhouetted against a broad river in the east. L'onee was speaking again:

"I almost flew to Khotahay yesterday instead of to—" The name she spoke was lost in the shouting of the wind. "I was in a panic after failing to locate you at any of the twelve bridges that cross the river of boiling mud. Time and again I tried to cross myself, and when I finally could, I knew that you had broken the sixth spell and that I had missed you. I knew all the while that I couldn't possibly keep an accurate watch on so many crossings.

"I was captured as I flew over the city, but, of course, I didn't mind. I had taken care to locate the central fort, and I immediately possessed the body of an important woman servant inside it. From her it was an easy jump at the proper time to the body of Calya, the Nushir's blond wife."

Holroyd listened to the explanation with but half his attention. The picture she had drawn filled little gaps in the continuity of her life stream since he had last seen her. But, staring now at the nearing capital, his thought leaped ahead. Ineznia was down there. And the chair of Ptath.

It was hard to imagine her. The intense, passionate creature that was the golden-haired goddess seemed unreal, up here in this night, with a whining wind tearing at his flat-held body, with the great, dark wings of the mighty animal he rode rising and falling in a repetition of violent movement.

The god chair evoked no image at all. His mind refused even to grope for a mental picture. But it must exist down there! L'onee believed it; and Ineznia had planned everything on the certainty that the chair was a reality. Long ago, Ptath must have told them of it. It was possible, of course, that he had misled them, but that was a dangerous assumption.

"If I had been Ptath—" Holroyd thought, and then smiled with a savage consciousness of the incongruity. He *was* Ptath. At least, there wasn't any other. "If I had been Ptath," he repeated, "and I had mistrusted one of two women—or both, to play safe—I would not have left my main protective to any kind of chance at all. No matter what was done to it,

I'd have tried to figure something—something designed to shock, or frustrate, any schemer alive. I wouldn't just have left it a straight business of sit in the chair or else!''

Down swooped the screers, screaming. Lights flickered below; and in the glow a great courtyard was revealed. One by one the birds came down and made their separate runs like massive aircraft settling onto a landing field.

Men bowed low as Niyi's face was recognized. There was a scramble to help them with the removal of furs and a rush to open doors.

"Do not," commanded L'onee-Niyi, "awaken the palace. The Nushir's guest and I shall proceed without escort."

There were soldier guards at intervals along the gleaming corridors who sprang to attention, great bearded men who looked strange in neat uniforms, and who stood very stiff, as the man and woman strode past. Holroyd whispered finally, "Do you know where she is? Where the chair is?"

He felt tense and excited, realizing that the crisis of his life was upon him.

Beside him, L'onee whispered, "I know exactly where it is. After all Niyi knew and—there it is—the door at the end of this corridor."

It was a big, ornamental entrance, and it was locked. Holroyd tested his strength against its solidity. The hardwood shook and quivered from the smashing blow, but did not splinter.

"Wait!" L'onee said urgently. "There's no doubt she's inside. But I'll have the guards break the door." She finished with satisfaction. "This time we have the authority. There's not a body in the palace that she could usurp, and overrule Niyi. I—"

She stopped and said softly, "Ah!"

The door was opening in a leisurely fashion. Ineznia stood there just across the threshold. She had on a black gown that made her hair like a golden crown set above dark velvet. She was smiling and she said:

"Enter. I've been expecting you."

CHAPTER XIX

Battle Of The Goddesses

THE BLUE EYES OF THE GODDESS INEZNIA SPARKLED WITH tiny yellow flashes and her smile waxed and waned, as if her joy was coming to her in wave on wave of flooding happiness. She spoke again, a variation of her first words:

"I've been watching for you. But of course, without water it is impossible to tell an *essence* when it is in a body. Come in, both of you. I shall be glad to tell you all about everything."

Her victorious mood seeped into Holroyd's mind. Smiling grimly, he stepped forward and halted, teetering on his toes as Niyi's voice rang with L'onee's warning:

"Ptath—wait! There's something wrong."

Holroyd recovered his balance, then stood very still. There was no fear connected with the paralysis, simply a great wonder, and the earlier sense of unreality grew stronger. The unemotional conviction came that he was dreaming. After a minute, however, he was still standing there, studying that delicate face with its flickering smile. Girlish women, he thought grimly, were not good-looking when they gloated. Once more the goddess spoke:

"How melodramatic we are, L'onee. Of course there is something wrong—the wrongness of defeat. What! You still hesitate? I assure you we shall not be disturbed. And you really *must* have a look at the chair that would have won for you had you arrived six hours ago."

Said the spider to the fly, Holroyd was thinking, won't you please come in? The reference to the chair scarcely touched him. Instead, his mind absorbed itself in a contemplation of why Ineznia should be so sure they would not be disturbed. It was particularly odd as, out of the corner of his eye, he saw that a number of women were coming along the corridor. A shocked thought came. Holroyd whirled on L'onee.

"It's just struck me that I've seen neither of you in possession of a man's body. Can—"

L'onee had been standing, frowning, as if she were searching for something that kept eluding her. Now, she looked up.

"Only women, Ptath, or female animals. There is a physical law involved that—"

She stopped and stared as Ineznia crumbled to the floor. Then she cried shrilly, "Ptath. She's gone to someone's body."

The women were behind her now, and close. One of them was fumbling under her dress. A razor-thin stone knife flashed; and Holroyd, smiling with a savage understanding, caught L'onee—and took the flung knife in his side. Still smiling, he jerked it out. He flicked a glance toward Ineznia; the goddess showed no sign of life. She was still one of the five women, and she could shift to any of them. He felt a stark and gathering consciousness of the danger that was here.

"Quick, L'onee," he urged, "order the women to go away at once. The one that is dominated by Ineznia will try to kill Niyi, and thus drive you into a less authoritative body. *Hurry!*"

Her understanding must have been quicker than his words. Her voice was ringing out in sharp command, cutting across his words. Obediently, three of the women began to walk back the way they had come. One of the remaining two stood uncertain, but the other shouted:

"Come back here. This is not Queen Niyi, but an imposter. The queen is with our master, the Nushir, at the border, as we all know."

The speaker was a powerful-looking creature, obviously a woman's superintendent of some kind. In response to her command the three who had been leaving, faced about, looking very frightened, and one of them called in a trembling voice:

"If this is so, why not call the guards?"

L'onee whispered from the shelter of Holroyd's body, "What shall I do? Call the guards myself?"

Holroyd hesitated. His brain wouldn't concentrate on the immediate threat. It kept flashing off in tangents, reaching out to grasp the larger meaning, the potentialities of what he was seeing. He had never realized it before, but what a terrible power it was that Ineznia and L'onee possessed, this ability to shift from body to body. They could enter anywhere, palace, fort, anywhere where there were women and instantly kill right and left. The confusion would be absolutely devastating. Nothing could possibly resist such demonic personalities. Entire fortifications must fall without a fight, in an insane cataclysm of fratricidal murder or self-inflicted death.

It was suddenly clear that the days of Nushirvan as a separate state were numbered. Its long immunity was shattered now that Ineznia could cross the river of boiling mud at will. Just why she hadn't long ago dominated the colossal land of Accadistran, which was apparently not protected, was something he would have to find out, but the immediate danger was right here, and now!

What had happened was, of course, utterly clear. L'onee and he had arrived before Ineznia had accomplished her purpose. In spite of all her advance confidence, she hadn't been able, in the short time available, to negate the power of the god chair. She must have known a great fear when she heard his body smashing at the door. But her recovery had been abnormally swift. Instantly she had laid her plans, occupied the body of an important woman and sent these women along this corridor. Then, returning to her own body, she had come to the door and skillfully stalled for time. Here was the result: Five women, who, if properly handled, might be used successfully to destroy L'onee's body.

Afterward, all the uncontrolled witnesses could be killed, or forced to kill themselves. The one that remained would swear that Holroyd murdered Niyi and, once under such a charge, and in prison, he'd have the devil's own time getting back to the room of the god chair. In the interim, Ineznia expected to accomplish her aim.

It was a pretty though desperate scheme, pitiful when compared to the five billion soldiers she could muster to do her will in Gonwonlane, but deadly for all that, and not to be fooled with.

Holroyd hissed at L'onee, "Yes, call the guards. After all, we can prove that you're Niyi by the escort that brought us from the border."

In a minute the guards had the women. And there was not even an attempt to pretend that L'onee was not Niyi. As he had analyzed, her whole plan had been adopted on the spur of the moment, under the pressure of unexpected events.

L'onee was commanding, "Lock these women in their rooms, but release them in the morning. I will take occasion at some later period to reprimand them for their insolence."

One of the guards glanced at the knife in Holroyd's hand, but all he did was point at Ineznia, who was rising to her feet; he said:

"What about her?"

L'onee smiled; said coolly, "She's a victim. Let her be."

A moment later the three of them were alone. The two women, Holroyd saw, were staring at each other. And only L'onee was smiling. He was about to step past them and enter the room when the silent intensity of that eye interchange penetrated to his consciousness. He paused and glanced from one to the other, puzzled. It was L'onee who broke the silence. She said in an unnatural drawl:

"We-e-l-ll, darling Ineznia, so you've overreached yourself in spite of all your scheming."

Her smile faded; she snapped: "Just a moment, Ptath, until I examine the threshold of this door. If she's managed to lay protective metal here anywhere we—"

She fell to her knees and pushed her fingers cautiously along the carpet. When she came to the door, Ineznia stepped forward with a swift movement and viciously kicked at her hand. Deftly, laughing softly, L'onee caught the thrusting foot. Her lips twisted savagely; with all her strength she pushed. Holroyd gasped as the delicately built Ineznia went spinning back into the room. She caught her balance, started forward again, then stopped with a convulsive effort, her face contorted with anger. It struck him for the first time how inconceivably violent was the hatred of these two women for each other.

Ineznia hissed, "When the six months are up, I shall destroy you a little piece at a time."

L'onee laughed, a brittle laugh. "So I have six months, have I? Thank you, my sweet, for telling me." Still laughing in that brittle fashion, she turned to Holroyd. "So far as I can make out, there's nothing to hinder us going into the room."

She came to her feet and her laughter was a glowing thing

as she said, "Oh, Ptath, Ptath, there's victory here; and all because she grew frightened at my escape."

Holroyd's puzzlement must have shown in his face, for L'onee explained swiftly:

"Her original intention was that you should attack Nushirvan, and thus cross the river of boiling mud. Moving with the army over those mountains, it would have taken you weeks, perhaps months to reach this palace. And during all that time she could have been studying the chair in this room, and I'm sure she could have destroyed it under such circumstances.

"But that ring I gave you startled her. It was only Ineznio's seal ring, but when I was in the writing room getting it, I put some of my power into it. She recognized that as a declaration of war, and rather than give me time to be a nuisance to her, she acted as she did."

L'onee laughed again, the slightly harsh but gleeful laugh of Niyi. Ineznia stood without moving just inside the chair room. Her face was the color of chalk, but her eyes were blue and cold and deadly as she said:

"You realize, I hope, that you at least will die, L'onee. Any power Ptath may derive from the chair is not *full* power. Only from prayer does power come, and I have long ago seen to it that that does not exist for him. And, furthermore, he will not be long in joining you in the dungeon."

She went on more airily, "He will perhaps have a little more power than you now possess." She laughed with an easy confidence, continued, "Now that I have resigned myself to this partial defeat, the rest doesn't matter. Once again I suggest to you the key word, Accadistran."

"You devil beast!" said L'onee.

They stood very still, the dark woman and the golden woman, staring at each other. And, glancing first at one, then the other, though he understood only dimly what they were discussing, Holroyd had the sudden conviction that he oughtn't to be here. He oughtn't to be seeing the naked souls of these women.

It cost him an effort to break the thrall. He shook himself—a mental and physical movement it was—and stepped across the threshold into the large room. He was aware of L'onee following, of Ineznia turning to watch. Then he forgot them both.

CHAPTER XX

The God Chair

THE ROOM IN WHICH HOLROYD FOUND HIMSELF WAS, EXCEPT for the chair, unfurnished. It was built entirely of stone, floors, walls, ceiling, all unalleviated stone. Gray stone, it was, uncracked, yet in spite of this the effect was of great, of incredible age. The room was *old*.

The chair occupied a portion of the room to Holroyd's left. It shone. It was so bright it hurt his eyes. It was an enormous misty structure, insubstantial and quivery. Veins of crystal light glittered in it; opalescence clouded its surface; splashes of amber streaked it, and bands of vermilion interlaced with stains of pallid ochre. It glittered like some intricate jewel, and its shape was that of a perfect cube with dimensions of fifteen feet. It floated above the floor. It tantalized; it entranced. It had no relation to the solid realities all around. Holroyd walked toward it, then stood in a maze of fascination, staring up at it. It was distinctly *up*. The lower surface of the cube flickered at least ten feet above his head.

He found himself, automatically, looking around, searching for something that would enable him to climb and sit on the great, glowing "seat". The action of looking brought awareness of the two pairs of eyes that were staring, *glaring*, at him. Two pairs of eyes, each pair ablaze with its own excitement. Two pairs of eyes expecting a god to be born.

It was hard to break the hypnotic hold of them, but Holroyd shook his head slightly and it was as if a rock had fallen into the glassy pool that was his mind. The widening ripples broke the spell. He saw, then, that stone rungs were carved into the stone wall to the left of the chair. Up they ran, straight to the ceiling and *along* the ceiling. They ended above the chair. By climbing up he could swing himself by his hands from rung to rung, and drop directly down onto the chair. An athletic child could have done it without a second thought. The One Who Is Strong should do it without a second thought. But the second thought, the hesitation, came even as he walked slowly toward that ladder of chiseled stone.

The thought had nothing to do with his will to sit in the chair. He was going to sit in it. There was no alternative. Even if he had had proof that the goddess had managed to tamper with it, he would still have had no alternative but sooner or later to test the effect of it upon the body of Ptath. No, there was no question at all about that. He must sit in the god chair. Only it was clear now that it wouldn't be enough. In a way, he had known from the first moment he had learned that god power came from prayer that the chair alone would not be enough to make him Ptath, the Thrice Greatest.

The chair was at most the firing cap, a detonator. Or rather, it was a battery of stored power that would start him off with power which could later be replenished and increased from the source of god power itself—the prayers of billions of women. Prayers cunningly suppressed by Ineznia. And not likely to be resumed in any measure during a conceivable period of time. Religious habits had in their texture a conservatism unmatched by any other human institution.

He began to climb up the stone ladder, but he was thinking: The victory he was about to gain would be defensive. His own life would be saved, but L'onee would die, and the soul-destroying temple civilization would go on and on.

He had a sudden sense of futility. He glanced over his shoulder at the two women standing there, eyes fixed upon him. Hard to imagine they had once been his wives. The passionate and ambitious golden-haired child woman, the dark, intense L'onee. How did he know her real body was brunette? He had not seen her since his arrival in Gonwonlane. Yet he knew.

Perhaps it was because he was swinging, hand over hand along the ceiling, and the chair was nearer. Nearer; then it was directly below. It shone up at him like a great mirror that gave off a shimmering jewel light of its own. In a moment he would be a god.

Blankly, he hung there, looking down. Then he dropped. Instantly, he sat down. And began to sink *into* the cube. He vanished. Long minutes passed. His leg protruded first from the bottom. He fell to the floor sixteen feet below. The cube shimmered for a moment. Then made a faint *poof* sound, and was gone, like a burst soap bubble. On the floor Holroyd lay without movement, like a dead man.

The silence was broken by the tinkling laughter of Ineznia. L'onee twisted with a jerky movement to stare at the golden goddess. Her eyes widened as she saw the unalloyed glee in the child face. With a little cry she stumbled to the still body that lay on the floor, half fell, half flung herself beside it. She tugged and pulled at the dead weight of Holroyd until he lay on his back. She put her fingers to his eyes, opened them. They closed limply as she withdrew her trembling hand. The laughter of Ineznia rang maniacally in her ears as, one by one, she forced herself to touch the life spots of the still body.

Color crept back into her cheeks. "He's still alive!" she breathed. And knelt there, conscious of a gathering bewilderment. Behind her, the other's laughter ended on a mocking note.

"Of course, he's still alive," Ineznia said. "I wasn't able to find a single death energy in the entire structure of the chair. It's the purest complex of positive forces ever conceived. My intention was to find some method of destroying it as he has now done."

There was a complacency in the golden goddess' tone as she finished that brought to L'onee a terrible exasperation. She twisted around, raged:

"Don't pretend that you had anything to do with it!"

"I am pretending nothing," Ineznia said coolly. "I'm as surprised as you are. But of course, now that it's happened, it is quite obvious what took place."

It wasn't obvious to L'onee. If it had been she felt very sure that she would have had an advance inkling and prevented the catastrophe. She parted her lips to ask for an explanation. But one look at that avid, delicate face brought abrupt memory that Ineznia never answered questions. She boasted. It didn't take long.

"It is clear," Ineznia said in a matter-of-fact tone that only partially concealed her exultation, "that Ptath never intended to experience the power of the chair until he already had *in* him the full weight of the prayer power. Lacking that insulation, he has been temporarily burned out." She frowned. "A comparison is difficult to make, but it would surprise me if he was ever again capable of becoming a pole of power.

"Why did he need the chair at all if he expected to have already in him the power of the prayers of billions of women? That is even more difficult to answer, but it is well to remember that Ptath intended always to remain greater than any possible combination we might form against him."

Ineznia shrugged gracefully. Watching her, L'onee thought that the goddess-ruler was having a special difficulty of her own, the difficulty to keep from shouting with happiness. The woman glowed. She made little, quick movements with her fingers, and even her body seemed to shiver, as if thrill on thrill of ecstasy was coursing through it. Her whole being was alive with joy. It was amazing that she could keep her voice so calm, so reasoning as she went on:

"Naturally, even though he has ceased to be a danger to me, I shall take no chances. I will transport him now to my great capital, Gadir, in Accadistran, and let him go the way of all Gonwonlanians who have been kidnaped."

Her laughter rang like metal clashing with stone, so hard was the sound of it. "It will be interesting to see what happens when a god body is torn to pieces. After that"—she paused tantalizingly—"as soon as those fool rebels launch their attack on Nushirvan, I shall order my sky riders to act."

L'onee stared at Ineznia whitely. Twice, she tried to speak, but each time only managed to swallow her horror. Ineznia laughed, then said with a ringing savagery, "Don't try to tell me that it isn't necessary. There's only one kind of union that Gonwonlane will ever accept with Accadistran—the union of crushing defeat."

She added, almost as an afterthought, "And while my war flyers are about it, I shall see to it that every prayer stick in Gonwonlane is their loot. I'll take no chances. I'll let the praying of the Accadistrans support my power until the last possibility of woman-praying is stamped out of Gonwonlane. Ptath, of course, will be long dead by then."

She was silent; her eyes were starry, her face gentle as she mused finally, aloud, "I haven't decided yet on the type of government I will set up when the last wrinkle of resistance has been erased. The temple system has weak as well as good points, as witness the large number of rebels in existence under its aegis. Those insolent scoundrels, daring to oppose me!''

Once again she was silent; then grimly, ''I *cannot* brook opposition. Except for that, and if I had the old Ptath's ability to co-ordinate the actions of masses of men, I might even be tempted to restore the curious type of government that he tolerated. I never did quite understand its inner meaning, but it was very exciting until after he departed, when it became quite unruly and intolerable. You will remember, L'onee, darling, that was the first time I overrode you and, actually, it was the result of our quarrel at that period which finally convinced me that a government of two sovereign goddesses was an unendurable paradox.''

In a vague way, as the other talked, L'onee had been aware that Ineznia was edging closer. Now she realized the goddess' intention. She turned, straightened—too late. Ineznia flung herself onto Holroyd's body and clung there while L'onee struck and tugged at her frantically.

''Watch out, you fool,'' Ineznia breathed furiously, ''or you'll come along.''

She *couldn't* let the warning matter. She felt the change. Without water it was a slow process, a straining, but after minutes there was movement through darkness. Almost instantly, she was lying on hard ground; and it was day.

CHAPTER XXI

The Zard Of Accadistran

SHE HAD A SENSE OF TERROR NOT HER OWN. IT GREW OUT OF the sobbing and moaning of women, the crying of children, the high-pitched voices of men. Countless women and children and men clamorous with horror and fear. The terrible sound brought knowledge of where she was. Not that she had been in doubt.

L'onee stood up, searched hastily with her eyes and sighed with relief. Of Ineznia there was no sign. But Ptath lay on a cot that rose level with her knees. He looked dead. He lay without movement or twitching of any kind, without indication of returning consciousness. L'onee sent her gaze again wearily to take in her surroundings.

Ptath and she were inside a walled enclosure. The enclosure was about a kanb square, and it was packed with humanity. In the distance beyond one great line of wall she could see the trained screers of the Zard wheeling and flying, formation after formation diving down out of sight. She shuddered with horror of what was happening out there. Here, in one of thousands of training areas for screers, was the dead end for the kidnaped of Gonwonlane.

Her gaze came back from distance. She saw for the first time that the cot on which Ptath lay was in a special, fenced off area. The area was thick with other cots, on every one of which sprawled one or more human beings. Individuals would get up and wander dazedly off, but always others would be brought in to fill the vacant spaces. Children, men, women.

L'onee sat down on the edge of Ptath's cot and waited. She thought desperately: Ineznia wouldn't delay, not now. She'd have Ptath killed the moment it could be managed, whether he was conscious or unconscious. First of all, she'd take the true Ineznia body back to the city of Ptath—she wouldn't risk *that* in a city where metal was reasonably common. Then she'd send her essence back to the palace at Gadir, enter the body of the woman Zard of Accadistran, and give the necessary orders. As fast as screers could fly and grimbs run, soldiers would rush to obey them.

In a surge of panic she caught the still body and shook it violently. "Wake up, Ptath!" she cried in a low voice. "Wake up!"

The body did not stir. It lay in a deathlike trance, limp beneath the clutching fingers of her hand. If he was really beyond aid, then she ought to leave him, leave this body of Niyi, and go back to Nushirvan. There were things that she could do, even little things might help to prevent the cataclysm of terror and death that Ineznia was planning. She mustn't stay here when continents trembled on the brink of doom.

Still she hesitated. The sun, which had been low in the east, tilted toward a mid-morning position. The dust of a half million restless feet thickened the air like a gray mist. The day grew hot, then stifling. Two men trudged toward her carrying a third man. One said:

"There doesn't seem to be a cot for my brother."

The other man lowered the head and shoulders of the unconscious one. He said wearily:

"What does it matter? He's going the way of the rest of us."

"I'll get a cot," said the first speaker quietly. "My brother's in a bad way. He—"

He saw that he was talking to a retreating, unheeding back. He broke off. Then he came over to L'onee.

"I hope you don't mind if I move him"—he pointed at Holroyd—"off the cot. My brother is unconscious."

L'onee stared. The demand was so outrageous that she thought she hadn't heard it correctly. Then she parted her lips to speak, but before she could utter the scathing words, the man bent forward and started to lift Holroyd from the cot.

She caught his arms and pushed him. His fingers clutched her arms as he stumbled back, jerked her to her feet. He was strong and there was a blind, stubborn will in him. Her only thought was to shove him, and that was like pushing a heavy weight. In a minute the body of the Nushir's pampered first wife was utterly exhausted. She was half leaning against the man when his whisper beat into her ears.

"Go to Nushirvan!" he hissed. "Go to Nushirvan! I'll meet you there in the Khotahay palace—later."

L'onee froze. Then she shook the man in a frenzy of incredulity, but he was staring at her suddenly with a gathering blankness that changed to shock and horror. He gasped:

"I must have been mad. I don't know what got into me. I'm sorry."

She was too exhausted even to feel pity. She staggered back toward the cot, started to sink down on it and straightened in dismay. Ptath's body was gone.

The tremendous shock faded after a long minute. Understanding poured through her. She should have realized the instant the man spoke those words about Nushirvan. Ptath had thought it possible all these hours that Ineznia might be in a nearby body watching. He didn't want Ineznia to know that he could transfer himself from body to body. He didn't want Ineznia even to suspect that he was the god Ptath and so he had caused a distraction and slipped away.

"If you don't mind," said a familiar man's voice, "I'll put my brother on this cot now."

L'onee glanced sharply at the tired face. But the fellow's expression showed no sign of what she was looking for. There was no reason, of course, why it should. The man had served Ptath's purpose. And she had her instructions. *Go to Nushirvan!* Still she stood there hesitating because Ineznia must be convinced, utterly convinced, that she was safe forever.

The thought was like a flashed signal. There was a movement on the high wall to her right, then to her left. Ladders with soldiers swarming down them. In a half dozen minutes they had overflowed the "hospital" area, blocking the gates, lining up along the "hospital" fence. Ruthlessly, they pushed cots out of the way, knocking them over, human contents and all. Great light-saws were brought into action. The main wall began to crumble. In not more than ten minutes a fifteen-foot-wide gap had been cut clean through the thirty-foot-high main wall. Through the gap rode a woman mounted on a monster grimb.

The woman was tall and slender, yet of commanding build.

Her brown eyes were bright, almost amber in their glowing intensity. Her face was lean, finely formed, and proud. For L'onee, the lines of pride alone would have identified that glorious creature. Physically, Ineznia had made an unsurpassable selection. The woman Zard of Accadistran looked every inch a queen, fully capable of carrying off her great role as ruler of more than twenty billion subjects. The question was, was Ineznia in possession of the body now?

The grimb halted. Soldiers rushed forward carrying a set of glittering steps, down which the woman Zard walked with an easy grace. Smiling bleakly, she walked over to L'onee, where the latter stood beside the cot that Ptath had occupied such a short time before. She glanced at the man lying on the cot, started to face L'onee, and then twisted back to the cot, her eyes becoming wide and awful.

She started to speak, then she made a gesture with her hands, a crazy, scratching gesture toward the face of the stranger who lay on the cot, as if she would change those alien features by violence into the shape she had expected to see. With a visible effort she restrained herself, whirled, and cried in a low, intense voice:

"Where is he, you incredible fool? He was here a few minutes ago."

Now, thought L'onee, *now*, this minute, she must convince this maddened ruler that her own false analysis of what had happened to Ptath in the god chair was correct. Trembling, she parted her lips to utter the words that would give Ineznia the great personal satisfaction that, in all the long years of L'onee's imprisonment, she had striven to gain.

Abruptly, briefly, it was impossible to say them without some preliminary that would make the plunge into ignominy easier. Shakily, she said:

"So you've run into the old difficulty, Ineznia, that even a goddess cannot be in two places at once."

It was instantly simpler to take the next step. She went on wearily, "Well, it doesn't matter. When he wakened up, I thought I'd give him the same chance as these other poor wretches. I sent him out into the crowd. Ineznia—"

She paused, her face contorted with the effort of her will. She thought: You proud fool, this is life or death. The very fact that Ptath doesn't want Ineznia to know proves that he hasn't got enough power to damage her. He needed time to plan, to think. No matter what the cost, she must see to it that he got it. She said in a thick, choked voice:

"Ineznia, I beg you, do you understand, I *beg* you not to launch this unnecessary war. You've won. If you want Accadistran and Gonwonlane to form a mixed race, you can do it in a dozen normal ways; intermarriages, forced if you must, but without mass murder. Ineznia, please, please do not launch this war."

She saw that the brown eyes of the woman, that had been like violent pools a minute before, were changing—*the* change that was so vital. Sardonically now, those eyes stared at her; the mocking voice of Ineznia the Zard came:

"Poor L'onee! As ever you are incapable of rising above your humanness. There is locked in your words, and not very securely locked, an hysteria verging on the sentimental. Know, my dear, that a goddess must be like the wind, which transports the evil odors as impartially as it bears the fragrance of a field of flowers. I assure you I am not being wilfully cruel. It is simply that alien peoples do not merge naturally, and I now decree that the days of separate nationalities are over. So shall it be."

L'onee said drably, "This is what Ptath feared in the old days; it was what he saw growing within himself: A remorseless impatience with human weakness, a ruthless disregard of the race from which we, all three of us, were originally sprung. It was to prevent that beast god from appearing that he merged himself with the race. He—"

She stopped as she saw that the woman was not listening. The woman Zard, whose body Ineznia occupied, had turned and was staring out into the mass of humanity that milled sluggishly in the vast enclosure beyond the stone "hospital" fence. Ineznia said slowly:

"So he's out there, is he? Well, he can't escape. No one ever has. I'll have Ineznio's portrait shown to all the guards at the chute, and when *his* turn comes I'll be notified. I want personally to see him die." She faced L'onee, a twisted smile on her lips. "You will be glad to know that this morning I gave the order for the attack on Gonwonlane. Nothing that anybody can do can stop the forces I have now set in motion, so ponderous are they. Even I couldn't stop them." Her smile grew savage. "We shall now see what happens when one general in two bodies plans the strategical position of both armies. Well, good-bye, L'onee, darling. I'm saving your body for you. I want to destroy you and it together."

She whirled away, climbed the bright steps to the back of the grimb. In ten minutes, masons were at work filling the gap in the wall.

L'onee couldn't decide, not right away. She stood near one of the gates, fighting the impulse to rush into that human anthill. It would be useless, of course. Even Ineznia with all her will to find Ptath had taken a single look out over that sea of heads and realized the impossibility of locating one man. She mustn't do anything foolish. She must go to Nushirvan, do what she had originally planned—and wait for Ptath. Immensely important as was Ineznia's announcement of the war she had ordered, Ptath couldn't be told until he came to the rendezvous. What he would do when he did learn the truth, she couldn't imagine. The attack seemed final, decisive, all-conquering, capable of nullifying even a Ptath with prayer power behind him, which he didn't have.

A wave of hopelessness surged through her. Events were becoming too big for any one person. The attack was ordered, the culminating crime of a goddess' base scheming. By tonight the trained killer screers of the woman Zard would be flying across the narrow, old Sea of Teths. L'onee forced the image out of her brain, felt a brief pity for Niyi, whom she must leave behind, and then launched herself toward Nushirvan.

CHAPTER XXII

Within The Walls Of Death

IN SPITE OF THE INTERVENING COTS, HOLROYD COVERED THE distance from his own cot to the nearest gate in approximately five seconds. Reaching the gate, he pushed with relentless strength into the human mass that surged there at the edge of the "hospital" area.

One last glance he flung rearward. And saw that L'onee was still struggling with the man who had tried to put his brother in Holroyd's cot. No one else, particularly no woman, was moving. If Ineznia was there in some sick woman's drab body she was not revealing herself by the slightest untoward action. It *looked* as if he was safe.

He pressed on to make sure of it, and came after a little to more open ground. Instead of one human being to every square foot, there was one to every two feet. The difference was perceptible, but that was all. It was still like moving in quicksand, or in a heavy sea; no strength seemed adequate in itself. Nevertheless, the difference was there. It buoyed him up during the two fantastic hours that followed. Slowly, however, the shocked realization crept home that his plan, to find some place where he could safely leave his body, had no meaning in this restless ocean of human driftwood.

Noon came and passed. An hour later he was still struggling within a stone's throw of the same long-stretching main wall that formed, farther back, one flank of the "hospital"—pushing, fighting, at times surging helplessly with the crowd. Surely there were entrances or exits to this incredible concentration camp, gateways that would be guarded, naturally, but that didn't matter. He came, finally, to a man who looked more intelligent than frightened. Holroyd shouted, "How are we taken out of here? And where?"

The man stared at him blankly. Ten other men in succession gave him the same mindless look. It was like beating his head against the massive wall that loomed so enormous to his right. He ceased his pressure against the drift of the crowd. He let himself sway along like a leaf in a slow current, an eddying movement, assessing his position.

He had to find a place where he could be sure that his body would not be trampled. Physically, he was caught in this immense human trap, at least until he could find some guarded gate to the outside. His essence he could project, but bodily transport after the manner of Ineznia was not in his power. But now he was caught . . . caught in this monstrous mass of humanity. There must be some way out; there *must* be. He was starting forward again, determinedly, when he heard the bellowing voice.

It required a moment to locate the source of the voice. But abruptly he saw that a man was standing on top of the main wall fifty yards away, a man with a megaphone through which he was shouting. Before that sound the babble of the nearby crowd faded a little. Farther away, there was no diminishment, but after a moment Holroyd was able to make out what the man was saying.

"—Carpenters and men with ideas for killing screers should go to the carpenter's pit—over there beside the chute." The man pointed toward the far wall, then repeated his call. Beside Holroyd, a man said:

"It's a trick to get us nearer the chute. I'm staying right here."

The trick, Holroyd thought as he pressed in the direction the man had indicated, was much, much smarter than that. Victims thinking up methods to kill, or defend themselves from screers, so that the Accadistran general staff could devise training methods for the great birds under the most trying conditions.

The carpenter's pit should be an ideal place from which, tonight, to launch his essence to Nushirvan. Meanwhile, it wouldn't hurt to learn a few things about killer screers in action. It took less time than he expected to reach the far wall. The pack was not so tight during the last quarter kanb. A sprinkling of brave men and women loitered casually in the area around the chute, but the end result of their bravery was that they went first. Swarms of powerful men rounded them up into groups of a hundred and herded each group toward a hole in the towering wall. Always it was the powerful men who came back through that chute. And if the victims screamed in their agony out there, the sound was not audible above the uproar here of the victims-to-be.

Holroyd could see finally what seemed to be the carpenter's pit; an inclosure with high walls built against the main wall, and extending through or under the main wall out to the far side. Twice, as he headed for it, spearmen tried to include him in a hundred-group. Shamelessly, and at reckless speed, he sprinted aside, threading through the thinning crowd. There was a mob in front of the pit gate, from beyond which came the sound of wood and stone hammers. Individual resentments flared as Holroyd pressed toward the gate. Sharp cries came:

"Get back in line!" "Wait your turn!" "I'll punch you one!"

Blows came, and violent counter-shoves, but his strength was like a machine-driven steel bar. In five minutes he was at the gate. A dozen powerful men stood there, half of them armed with stone-tipped lances, half with bows that had arrows ready-thrust against gut strings. They wore headbands with feathers in them; and the one with the most feathers— four, Holroyd counted them meticulously—must be the chief officer.

In a flash of power tension he projected his essence at the commander. There was a sense of a ferocious personality resisting—then:

"That man next!" he cried in a deep voice and pointed at his own body which stood tall, lean, tan-faced, skillfully propped among several other pressing bodies. He waited until two spearmen caught the Ptath body; then he was back inside it and into the carpenter's pit.

The carpenter's pit was about two hundred yards square. And, just as he had observed, it extended *under* the massive main wall, projecting about a hundred yards out into whatever was beyond. Holroyd paused to let his mind absorb the overall picture. There were benches, rows of them, with one or two men working at each bench. They seemed to have endless supplies of wood and stone, which was natural enough, if the Accadistran military organization was co-operating. Their tools were great pots of glue and wooden light-saws.

Holroyd watched, fascinated, as a man at the nearest bench touched one of the light-saws to a stone. The instrument had no effect at all on the wielder's fingers, but it sheared through the stone like a hot knife cutting butter. He had first seen the remarkable tools in the service depots of the Gonwonlanian army. Then, he hadn't dared show any special interest. Now, he didn't have time.

As he turned to move on, a thickset man hurried toward him. "You're new, eh?" the man said briskly. "This way, please. We'll show you what we're fighting, then put you to work. Here's your number, 347."

The number was on an armband, which the man tied swiftly around Holroyd's left arm above the elbow. He went on earnestly, "Don't lose that. Don't let anyone tear it off. Any person who won't work, or who is found without a number at the moment when we're called upon to provide a victim, goes first. Otherwise, it goes by number." He finished, "There's two hundred of us here. And, except for the boss up there, we make a complete turnover every two months. The difference between us and those others out there is that we get food three times a day; they get it only in the morning, and they never last longer than a month. We do go, mind you: No. 147 was with the last batch. Any questions?"

Holroyd found himself liking the man. He saw with a startled glance that the fellow's number was 153. Which meant that this was probably his last full day alive. Yet he looked cool, eager, intense.

"Good man," Holroyd said. "I like to see bravery in the face of hell. What's your name?"

"Cred, sir," said the man. He broke off roughly. "What in Nushirvan am I doing, calling you sir! Come along."

Smiling thinly, Holroyd followed. He had made no mistake in pretending to unconsciousness from the first moment that the power of the god chair dissolved into his body. He had been awake throughout the long process, intensely awake, like a beast with senses sharpened to an agonizing pitch. Only there wasn't, and hadn't been, any agony. And there was no beast. Just Peter Holroyd, Captain, U. S. tank corps, acquiring the peculiar and curious ability to project his essence anywhere.

It was a tremendous power; his earlier analysis of the Nushir's vulnerability to it had already convinced him of that. But by itself his own power of projection was inadequate to cope with Ineznia's control of government and with her ability to send her entire body through space.

And besides, in that first instant he had recognized that his previous logic was also correct. The chair was only a reservoir of stored power which, once used up, could only be replaced from the very fount of god power, in his case the praying of devout women. Instantly he'd realized he must practice duplicity. The conversation between Ineznia and L'onee in itself justified the entire deception. Never would the sealed lips of L'onee have been able to tell him so much. Not till then did the vague, grim plan form: So she was going to attack, was she? If he could stop that attack short of success, then Ineznia was doomed.

Wizard she might be, but one thing about people she had forgotten. Or despised. Or perhaps never known: Human nature! Human nature would defeat the goddess of earth *if*—

"Here we are," said Cred.

Holroyd saw that a tall, gray-faced, gray-eyed, gray-haired man stood at the parapet. The man turned as Cred said:

"Commander, this is a new one. I'm showing him."

"Good," said the old man listlessly. "Let him see!"

CHAPTER XXIII

Food Of The Killer Screers

AT FIRST, HOLROYD SAW ONLY SCREERS FLYING BACK AND forth over the great arena. There was an immense grandstand in the near foreground, crowded with men watching the spectacle. But that was only an environment, which he scarcely noticed. Swarms of screers, masses of screers. After a moment, Holroyd saw something else. Only one out of every ten of the great bird beasts had a rider on its back; yet they flew in unison, like planes in formation. Suddenly, as if they had received a signal, a group of ten broke off and dived toward the ground.

For the first time Holroyd saw that there were victims on the ground below the birds. A hundred men and women, mostly men, but the women were there. Cold, his mind like a metal shaft, his eyes forced to pitiless observation, Holroyd watched the drama unfold. The victims defended themselves. They had mushroom-shaped shields that they ducked under, and from which they poked at their voracious enemies with long lances. The birds evaded the lances with a trained skill and plucked the defenders from under their hopeless shelters, like robins pulling worms out of the ground. It was over in about four minutes. Instantly, hundreds of baby screers swarmed from aeries in a massive stone building far to the right and fell to feeding.

"They start them young on meat, don't they?" Holroyd said in a voice that was rock steady. The commander seemed not to hear, but Cred looked at Holroyd, startled. Before he could speak, Holroyd snapped savagely:

"Never mind! What I want to know is, who the devil devised those pitiful mushroom shields?"

Once more the astounded Cred parted his lips as if to say

something, but this time it was the gray-haired man who cut
him off, who said wearily:

"And may I ask what—"

He stopped. He had turned and now he seemed to see
Holroyd for the first time. His eyes widened. Then he shook
his head in a gesture of tremendous relief; then—

"Prince Ineznio!" he breathed. "Prince—Ineznio!" He
fell to his knees. Tears streaked down his leathery cheeks. He
caught Holroyd's hand and pressed rough lips to it.

"I knew it," he whispered. "I knew the goddess would
sooner or later send someone. I knew that this blasphemy
could not go on forever. Oh, thank the goddess, thank the
goddess!"

Holroyd forced himself to stand very still. It was hard
because there was a rage gathering in him, a rage so awful
that his body seemed to threaten to shatter. Until this instant
he had held himself almost as cold as the icy volcanic mountains of Nushirvan, so cold outside, yet so blazing hot inside
that his whole being trembled in a terrible, precarious balance
of forces. Now that balance was breaking.

Thank the goddess! What a monstrous obscenity. Thank
the goddess! Vile, lecherous, lascivious witch! Wretched
debauched, wanton, bloody, devil woman!

The mad fury faded, yielded to a great tenderness that had
in it a bleak knowledge that this commander's recognition
of—Ineznio—and his faith in the goddess, would be helpful
to his own plan.

He said gently, "Arise, marshal, and keep that faith alive
during the still-hard days ahead. The goddess has indeed sent
me—" he spoke the lie without a qualm—"and has granted
me great powers to deal with the hideous evil that is here."
He went on more urgently, "But surely, marshal, you have
evolved better defenses against those man killers than the
wooden umbrellas."

The marshal was straightening. It was amazing how his
face had changed. There were still tears, but he wiped them
away with an angry hand, and said in a ringing voice:

"I have, indeed, sir. I have, indeed. I've been here since
the beginning of the kidnaping of Gonwonlanian citizens,
seven years ago, and I have yet to let those out there"—he
made a contemptuous gesture toward the grandstand across

the arena—"see a single one of my good ideas in action. Look!" He raced down the steps into the pit, came up with a light-saw. "Here's a simple, one-man defense I've developed."

He sketched rapidly in the solid stone, cutting grooves with the point of the light saw. "It's a long, light, strong pole of the common gand wood, forked at one end like a V. The defender jabs the V over the screer's neck as it runs toward him, then instantly shoves the point of the stick into the ground. The flying screer is a very curious bird, not too bright, with a limited capacity for absorbing instructions. Those out there"—the officer waved a hand toward the sky—"have been trained to duck spear thrusts. If they fail, however, they push right on regardless, depending on their immensely tough leather breast skin and the almost enclosing bone underneath to protect them.

"Thus with the V pole, the screer will continue pushing forward, beating his wings. The combined effect of that will be to lift him up from the ground, exposing his soft underbelly to lance or arrow. There will be many deaths, of course, but as you can see, everybody will be able to manage some sort of defense. If you wish, I shall send some out with the next hundred-group."

"Send out two," said Holroyd. "It isn't that they can possibly retrain a billion screers, but there's another reason for caution."

It wouldn't do, he thought, for the goddess to connect his merging with the crowd with a new development in the defensive-offensive tactics of the screer victims. Lips slightly parted, teeth showing, he watched the two V-pole wielders kill four screers before they were attacked by several birds simultaneously and pulled down.

This was it. In an hour he was sure of it. It would be a heartbreakingly long time before anything could be done on the necessary scale; and there were other things to watch and learn of this commander's experience. But there was a limitation on that last also. Tonight he must escape. Every extra hour in this small area would give the goddess so much more time to locate him. And discovery would a fatal! Tonight it must be, perhaps when the food was brought in—but tonight!

CHAPTER XXIV

The Sea Of
Teths

A STRETCHER PREPARED IN ADVANCE FOR HIS BODY; A WARNING to Cred and to the commander to show neither surprise nor alarm; then entrance into the body of the chief officer in charge of the men who brought the food—that was the beginning. Quietly, Holroyd the officer directed that the stretcher be picked up. The two soldiers to whom he gave the order obeyed without a word, and the others said nothing.

There was a corridor, then, in a brightly lighted building that was thick with the odor of cooked food. The corridor divided abruptly in two, one branching off at an angle of forty-five degrees to the right, the other at the same angle to the left. Most of the men headed up the left corridor; but Holroyd directed the stretcher bearers to the right. They came presently to a door. As they were going down the stone steps outside into the thickening twilight, a multi-feathered officer stopped and stared at the body. He was parting his lips to speak when Holroyd's essence crashed into his mind.

The officer entered the building at a brisk walk and headed along the corridor toward an open doorway that Holroyd had noticed as he and his two carriers passed it a minute before. Men sat inside the room the door opened upon; they were drinking some pale purple liquid that could have been grape juice. He left the multi-feathered officer there at the table and flashed back into the mind of the other. The man, he saw, had waited there on the steps, too bewildered to organize himself. Under Holroyd's guidance, the fellow hurried along after the two trudging stretcher bearers.

They came to a long, wide, dim street that was flanked by a great wall. The sight of the barrier brought a thrill. The wall! The outer wall of the human slaughterhouse. With a shock he saw that soldiers were patrolling its base. One of them paused and was staring with curiosity at the still form of Ptath.

"Down that street!" Holroyd loudly directed the stretcher bearers who had paused questioningly. "There's a cart coming to pick up this offal."

He walked boldly ahead of the two men, examining his surroundings with quick yet measured glances. He was on a hill; the enormous arena was on a hill and to his right was open countryside. To his left, many roads were visible, with a scattering of houses along some of them. The roads ran straight downward into a solid section of city beyond which was a harbor that was alive with ships. The city spread and widened and grew enormous to the left, but Holroyd gave that part of it one glance and then pushed it out of his mind.

The harbor—by heading around the part of the city that was directly ahead—and that would take time—he could reach the harbor, take possession of a ship captain's body and—No, wait! He felt impatient with himself. Damn it, he was forgetting the supernal power that his new ability of essence projection gave him. Take a ship, indeed! Rather, capture a screer and fly to Gonwonlane in a few hours. This was no time for slow ships, or anything that would cause delay.

The thought ended as he saw that he and his bearers had come to a stretch of open countryside. Holroyd pointed to the shelter of a clump of trees. "Put the thing down there," he said; and dismissed the men. He watched the two walk off up the road with the casual unconcern of the low in rank who, having been commanded to do an expected job, feel relief that it is over.

As soon as the men were out of sight, Holroyd had the officer follow them. All the way back to the wall and into the building he remained with the officer; and then, and not till then, fell back to the Ptath body. Gingerly, he climbed to his feet and started down the hillside. It was growing darker; and here, in an almost open country where there were no light sticks, that would shortly mean a great deal.

He found himself wondering what the officer was thinking, doing. It must be queer to have been possessed; there must be an uneasy memory of dreamlike action. The fellow might even convince himself that the action had never occurred. Profoundly, Holroyd hoped so.

He turned up a side road at the far end of which he could see buildings that looked as if they might belong to a farm. The faint glow in the western sky receded even farther; in half an hour intense darkness settled over the land. One by one, Holroyd examined the outhouses. It was very dark, not a light showing from any of the buildings, but from one of the smaller buildings issued a faint stamp of movement, and the rasping of a beak opening and closing.

Holroyd manipulated the door mechanism of the screer pen and peered in. A pair of glowing eyes swayed around and stared at him. Bold, yet cautious, Holroyd went inside. The bird offered no resistance as he saddled it and put on the bridle—obviously it was a domesticated breed, a nonkiller. He led it outside. It kept trying to squat down for him to mount; and when he finally permitted it to do so, it clacked softly with eagerness and made a running leap into the air the moment he was seated. An enormous moon peered up over the eastern horizon as the screer soared out over the ridged and restless Sea of Teths.

Morning found the bird flying over a hilly, forested coast line. Unending hills and forests, or so it seemed after two hours of flight at a speed that couldn't have been less than a hundred miles an hour. If only, Holroyd thought finally, he could find some habitation, any kind of place where he could be sure that his body would not be molested while he projected his essence to far Nushirvan. After half an hour there was still nothing. With abrupt, sharp speculation, Holroyd eyed the back of the screer. By twining his legs in the stirrups and sprawling forward on that broad back, he ought to be as safe as he could be anywhere. Within a minute after that decision, his body was behind him.

Through the darkness he probed with his essence, letting the vastness of the visionless night envelop him. And after a while, he knew that this was different. The short journeys had been simple, a straightforward movement across a space of a few yards. This was different.

There was a distinct sensation of pushing himself forward, a *willing* of movement that in itself brought movement. Holroyd came to a halt and poised, searching intently, waiting for an impression. But there was no light, no sound, no pressure of any kind. The universe was made of black, empty silence. He was alone in a great void.

Hesitant, he let himself fall back into his body. Briefly, he lay quiet, then turned his head across the water toward where the isthmus of Nushirvan must be, and probed again.

After a long time he began to wonder how he would know when he had what he wanted. What was it Ineznia had said? That it was impossible to sense the presence of an essence when it was in a body. But then, she hadn't been out, searching, as he was—searching, probing through impenetrable night. Perhaps, Holroyd thought finally, he was too high in the air.

He willed himself downward. It was like falling into a well, but grimly he forced himself on. At last he felt something. A pressure; uniform in quality it was, and becoming stronger and stronger as he lowered himself, more cautiously now, toward it. Water?—he thought. But he couldn't be sure. Memory came for the first time of a quiet pressure of some kind during those moments when he had been heading for, or back from, the bodies he had possessed. It hadn't seemed important at the time; and besides, it was a much dimmer force. This was sharp, not altogether pleasant; the suggestion was that contact would be unwelcome, or violent in some way. It must be water. He was still over the Sea of Teths.

Confident again, Holroyd pressed on. He must have been very near land because only a few moments passed before he felt a difference. Land!

There was no stopping; mountains had to be covered, hundreds of miles still intervened between himself and the great city of Khotahay. He gauged the distance, lowered himself finally, experimentally, toward where a collection of very coarse, strong pressures indicated the presence of life. Straight toward the nearest of the pressures he flashed, and recoiled from a shock that was electric in its violence.

A woman! Careful, Holroyd thought ruefully. He approached the second pressure more gingerly, but there was no alien aura, no resistance. He entered. The body in which he found himself was that of a small town official. Holroyd lingered barely long enough to note that the town was twenty-five miles due north of the capital.

His second body was that of a soldier walking along a market street in downtown Khotahay. He had a brief, confused sense of colorful buildings, and a babble of sound; and then he had taken his bearings. His third body was in the palace of the Nushir. It was that of one of the Nushir's secretaries, a very big, mustachioed young man who knew that the Nushir was at that very moment in a nearby drawing room with his wife, Calya.

With his wife, Calya! Holroyd smiled as he forced the young man to walk along a corridor toward the door of the room. A minute later he was staring through the Nushir's eyes at a Calya who was saying earnestly:

"The important thing is that you organize your forts and your palaces on the basis that the women are kept in separate quarters, and are permitted no weapons of any kind. Simultaneously, send your plenipotentiaries to the great rebel Marshals Maarik, Dilin, Lagro, Sarat, Clayd and others. Offer them the return of all kidnap victims in transit through your country; explain that you dared not oppose the Zard of Accadistran knowing that she was also Ineznia, and—"

Holroyd cut in softly, "Better postpone those instructions, L'onee. I can only stay long enough to arrange a rendezvous with you where we can meet physically."

Having spoken, he smiled—and waited.

CHAPTER XXV

Rendezvous In Khotahay

L'ONEE'S REPLY WAS A SURPRISINGLY LONG TIME IN COMING. The eyes of the plump Calya filled with tears. Her hands trembled. She leaned forward in her chair and at last she whispered:

"Ptath!"

She stood up, came over to where he was standing, and caught his arm. "Ptath," she half sobbed. "Ptath, she's ordered the attack. Do you understand? She has ordered the attack."

"Good!" said Holroyd.

It must have sounded, in the voice of the Nushir, differently than he meant it. For the blond woman drew back, a shocked look on her face. Holroyd stared at her.

"Don't be a fool!" he said grimly. "Right now we can't stop anything she does, and besides, if my analysis is correct, she is playing right into our hands. We can feel sympathy for all those poor devils who are going to die, but we mustn't be rushed into precipitant action."

Swiftly, he went on, "Since the Nushir now knows our secret, it may be just as well to make clear exactly where he stands now and in the future. I hope, to begin with, he understands that a person who can plan the diabolical attack of Accadistran on Gonwonlane won't waste time or thought on the Nushir of Nushirvan.

"As for the rest, I want to make clear that he will remain alive until he dies of old age. There must be some change, however, in his government. I have in mind a limited monarchy, during his lifetime. After that I don't know. I can't quite see a parliament representing eighty or eighty-five billion people. The members, no matter how many there were, would be too far removed from the individual voter.

"Regional governments seem to be in order, and I see no reason why the Nushir's descendants shouldn't play a distinguished if not a stellar role. He can take that or leave it. I'm sure he'll have the common sense to take it."

Holroyd paused, conscious of L'onee's tragic gaze upon him. Abrupt sharp memory came, too, that his body was out there on the back of a great bird beast; and that, if he had considered it important to get it back before he knew about the attack, now it was urgent. He pictured it suddenly sighted by a squadron of the flying killer screers of the Zard. He said hastily:

"The important thing is for the two of us to get together physically. And to do that I need your help in finding out for me where exactly my body is."

He explained how he had flown due south from the farmhouse from which he had stolen the screer, out over the Sea of Teths, and then west along an uninhabited shore of Gonwonlane. L'onee cut him off:

"Why, of course. That's the great Ptath forest reserve east of the city of Ptath. If you follow your present course you should come soon to a bay where three rivers meet and flow into the old sea. Land on the south shore of the largest of the four or five big islands, and wait for me there. I shall come in the body which you first saw when I climbed the great cliff." She smiled wanly. "It is the only lawful, free body that I possess now."

She paused, then, "Ptath," she said quietly, "you have a plan? I mean"—she made a gesture with her hand—"a real plan, one whose purpose is the frustration and overthrow of Ineznia?"

"I have a theory," said Holroyd slowly, "and an unshakable faith in human nature. I have a defensive weapon that will save billions of lives. I have the ability to enter the mind of any man anywhere, including temple emperors; but if Ineznia manages to get hold of my real body before I am ready to act, it's all over for us. That's the only answer I can give you."

He saw that the blue eyes were searching his face anxiously, but the Nushir's plump cheeks couldn't have shown much expression for she said uncertainly:

"How long will it be before you act?"

Holroyd sighed. He wished she hadn't asked that question. It was too hard to answer. His first analysis of the time that would have to elapse varied between four and five months. In view of the fact that he had signed L'onee's death warrant, the execution to take effect in six months, part of which was already past, it *mustn't* be longer than five months. Actually, of course, it wasn't up to him, but suppose five months. Even thinking about that made him quail. In five months the killer screers of the Zard would make a shambles of northern Gonwonlane. Men, women, children would die by the hundred millions. Cities would fall to the invader amid scenes of horror that would be like the end of the world on a scale colossal beyond imagination.

But the possible extent of the disaster *couldn't* make any difference. Way back in 1944 people had learned that lesson. Horror must be ignored, unflinchingly faced; and patient preparation made for the hour when evil could be ended in one devasting and overwhelming blow.

Holroyd drew his mind clear of the terrible picture. He said quickly, "I'll see you at the delta and explain everything. Good-bye for now."

It was only ten minutes after he returned to his own body that he saw the silver glitter of the three rivers L'onee had described. Two days passed before L'onee joined him there.

CHAPTER XXVI

Invasion Of Gonwonlane

THE ISLAND WAS A GREEN, IDYLLIC WORLD. ITS HILLS AND glades were alive with small game; and in every patch of jungle were fruit trees with their fruit in different stages of development. In the timeless safety of the fastness of the island, the two of them, the gaunt, tanned woman and the tall, dark-haired man, hid their bodies. And waited for the flow of power to come to Holroyd, the power that would mean that women were praying, and that victory was possible. The days and the weeks passed.

The time was not wasted. They took turns projecting themselves into bodies in every part of the land, authoritative bodies, marshals, high zos and fezos, temple rulers and rebel commanders. It was a slow, slogging business, like trench warfare. The continent was too vast, there were too many people with sluggish minds and a way of life rooted in conservatism. There were too many men in remote cities who said shrewdly:

"But the goddess has sent no warning about a war with Accadistran. Where are the Imperial scroll announcements? You are not telling us the truth."

"The goddess has not warned us!"

She hadn't. Rumors spread like a disease; merchants whose intercity grimb and screer transports failed to turn up uneasily closed their stores and, with a middle-class gift for self-preservation, retired to their country estates. Refugees poured south, crying terror. But there was no word from the goddess. Somewhere, Holroyd pictured her, sitting smiling with a cool calculation, or perhaps laughing that tinkling laugh of hers.

Holroyd and L'onee were in Ptath on the night the megalopolis was victim. They stood on a hill that overlooked the sea and the city, occupying the bodies of a married couple, reading the poster that Holroyd had seen earlier in the day:

> This night no light must reveal the sacred city to the flying screers of the Zard. The disaster that has befallen our land is the result of yielding to the importunities of faithless rebels in their mad will to attack Nushirvan. Have faith in the goddess!

Have faith in the goddess! Oh, Kolla! Oh, Ptath! Holroyd said bitterly, "It's a wonder she didn't realize before that a blackout will help the invader and hinder the defense. We'll see a lot of those signs from now on, just before an attack."

L'onee drew deeper into the shadows of a doorway, but she said nothing. The darkness thickened; clouds raced through a moonless sky overhead. Below her, the city sprawled in the shrouding blackness, the first vague masses of buildings quickly blurred by the intense night. But the city was there, unseen yet palpable. Ptáth, the eternal. The city of light, ancient home of the Shining One, the god king of the ages. *That* Ptath in darkness! For the first time in all its tremendous history no light showed. Ptath had merged into the night, become formless like the hills to the west.

Slowly, L'onee came out of the greater darkness of the door way. The patches of stars that shone through openings in the clouds did queer, passionate things to her dimly visible face. She whispered:

"Can't we do something? Must we stand by like spectators? Ptath, the nine golden cities of the west have fallen. In the east, Lira, Galee, Ristern, Tanis and the forty-three cities of the northeast gulf; and all the land of the eastern seaboard; and, on the north tip, besides glorious Kaloorna—"

"And tonight the city of Ptath itself," said Holroyd in a monotone. "No, L'onee, we can do nothing at all. Even as it is, we shall have to act with the barest minimum of the necessary power on our side and—" He stopped. She saw his body grow tense. His shadow shape turned and he seemed to stare in a rigid fashion toward the north.

He said, "Listen!"

L'onee heard it then, too. Like a faint moaning wind that precedes a cyclone, only not like that at all. The immeasurably terrifying sound pierced out of the black sky to the north.

"Sc—r—r—r—e—e—e—r—r—r!
"Sc—r—r—r—e—e—e—r—r—r!
"Sc—r—r—r—e—e—e—r—r—r!"

The first sound was like a signal. Abruptly, the alien, terrible cry of the great voracious birds filled the universe. A hundred thousand, five hundred thousand, *ten million* flying screers shrieked from the midnight heavens; the night became a shambles of madness.

Afterward, when it was all over, and they were back on the island, Holroyd raged, "I'll break her into little pieces. I'll—" His fury quieted. Because actually he knew with a cold and deadly certainty exactly what he was going to do with Ineznia, the beast woman.

It was not all one-sided, the battle for Gonwonlane. More and more individuals and groups fought with V-pronged poles and spears and—the army was coming. Holroyd watched its ponderous progress eastward, watched some of its screer divisions as they raced ahead to protect cities and engage the invader. Sometimes they won a battle and held for a day, for a week, before the general staff of the invader detached and concentrated masses of killer screers that overrode every opposition.

In the history of warfare, it seemed to Holroyd, no army could possibly have suffered as much as did the Gonwonlanian. Its supply sources cut, it ran out of food for days on end. Great units of men went crazy with hunger and ate their grimbs and their screers, and glared longingly at each other's flesh. Twice, Holroyd saw men eating men.

And still there was nothing to do but wait, and *wait*, and WAIT. A dozen times they talked over their plans and their situation, the woman with the body that had been dead, and the man whose dark eyes glowed more fiercely each day from the horror of what he was seeing, and the gathering, terrible determination in his soul.

"It's really very simple, this business of god power," Holroyd sighed one night as they sat on the green, lush grass of their island. "At a certain point you can project the essence that is you; let us call it a soul. A little further on, your whole body can be transported through space. A little after that you can take someone else along. The next step beyond that is the ability to move through *past* time, slowly, in the immediate past but, with the help of another pole of god power, swiftly across to parallel points of one coil of time to another, the jumps being about two hundred million years.

"Interspersed with those are other powers, for instance that journey of minds that Ineznia took me on. The amazing thing to me is that the spells of Ptath turned out to be nothing more than hypnotism, ideas planted in both your mind and Ineznia's, and which even she, in spite of all her power, was unable to throw off.''

L'onee said softly out of the darkness, "The old Ptath knew the human mind. He discovered that no brain would hold firmly more than six commands—suggestions—over a great period of time. If you will think over the six he selected you will realize how carefully he made his choice.''

Holroyd nodded wearily, but he said nothing more that night. It was a month later that he broke a long silence between them with:

"This old Ptath of yours, what was he like? And why did he merge with the race? From all appearances, from all results, it was the greatest error he ever made.''

The gaunt woman shook her head, said in a strong voice, "Look at yourself, Peter Holroyd. You are the Ptath I knew, the old Ptath, the great, earnest, conscientious Ptath. Look at yourself, I say, and you will see Ptath as he was and''—she added in a low tone—"as he will be!''

Before Holroyd could speak, she went on more sadly, "As for merging with the race, in one sense that does seem to have been disastrous. But he said he could feel in himself dark, alien, inhuman urges that he must purge by a return to the spring source of decency—the life force of the people. If his fears were justified, if he would have become more evil, then what we are seeing is not disaster but a rebirth of hope. I swear to you that all that Ptath desired I can now see in you, the unegotistic knowledge of what is right, the determination that evil shall not flourish, the ability to adjust to and strike the enemy with her own weapons, and yet lose nothing of that will to goodness, suffer no taint, no diminishment of honest purpose.''

Almost breathless, she paused; then sighed the old question between them, "Ptath, do you feel stronger? Do you feel a *growing?*"

And as always, Holroyd answered with a grim satisfaction: "Yes . . . yes, I do!"

On the one hundred twelfth night that meant something tangible. The daily test worked. He could move his *body* through space. And on the one hundred thirtieth morning he could take L'onee along without the use of water as a catalytic agent. Afterward, they stood gazing at each other with eyes that were glowing yet grim. The hour for action had come.

CHAPTER XXVII

The Fall Of A Goddess

LIKE WRAITHS THEY MATERIALIZED IN THE DUNGEON WHERE L'onee's true body was chained.

It took time to transport the material they needed, the stone forge, the fuel necessary for the breaking of metal links. Light-saws didn't work on metal.

It took time to substitute the body of a dead woman they had found who, in the dim light, bore a resemblance to L'onee, and to arrange the chains to look as if they still bound her.

"It isn't," L'onee said, "as if my body is desperately important with so many greater issues at stake. Besides, in the long run you could make some other body, that I possessed, into a pole of power. But I'm sure she will come here. The moment she finds out you are alive she'll come here to destroy me."

"Don't be so brave and self-sacrificing," Holroyd chided. "Your body is important; that's why we're counting on her coming here some time after our first move against her. But now let's get this paraphernalia, and our bodies, into a side room. We'll need it, and them, again when our trap has closed. Leaving our bodies around is dangerous but—"

Next stop, he thought, the body of a high official in the palace at Gadir, Accadistran.

The man was standing gazing out of a window that overlooked the mighty capitol of Accadistran, when Holroyd entered his body. The city spread below. To Holroyd, who had seen too many cities too briefly, it was simply one more design of stone and marble. Out of the corner of his eye he saw that one of the women in the room was idly moving her fingers. Holroyd turned from the terrace and stared at her more directly. Unmistakably now, her fingers signaled:

"L'onee!" They had agreed that both must always be present in an emergency—to make sure.

Smiling, Holroyd walked over to the woman Zard and, as she grew aware of him, plunged a knife into her heart. It was a cruel and cowardly blow, but he held his mind hard on the millions of human beings who had been torn to pieces by screers. And knew that no matter how this Ineznia-dominated body was destroyed, the only important thing was that it was!

Beside him a man screamed, "Deld, you murderer!"

Holroyd made no attempt to defend the body he had possessed. The spear roared through him with a shattering violence. His brain vibrated with the horror of pain nerves shouting their anguish. Stunned, he withdrew from the dying body and entered the body of the Zard's chief minister, who was in the act of hurrying over, and who was exclaiming in dismay. Holroyd kept on with the exclamations for several seconds, then made his announcement:

"There will be an immediate emergency cabinet session. And, Marshal, call the general staff for consultation on the necessity of withdrawing our armies from Gonwonlane. Guards, clear all nonofficials out of the room except the Zard's brother and sister; particularly clear all women."

L'onee was the Zard's sister.

Only one woman tried to resist, and her resistance was brief. She cried out in a frenzy of defiance:

"Too late, L'onee, you're too late. You waited too long. In three more months all Gonwonlane will be occupied. And, right now, the first thing I shall do is go to the citadel palace and destroy your true body, you fool!"

"Woman," thought Holroyd in a terrible satisfaction, "you don't seem to realize that a man killed the Zard, and that he was not a puppet of L'onee." Aloud, for the benefit of the courtiers, he said, "She must be hysterical!"

L'onee, in the body of the Zard's sister, came over swiftly, whispered, "I never for an instant thought she wouldn't suspect that you were alive. It makes everything easier. She'll have to go to her body in the sealed room in the palace, then go down into the dungeon. We must get there before she does. These people can be left for the time being."

It was as swift as that. They waited in the darkness of the

dungeon in their own bodies. Waited for Ineznia. Abruptly, the room grew bright as the whirling shape materialized, and steadied. And stared at them.

"Why, darling Ineznia," L'onee said, "how good of you to come here just as we desired."

The blue eyes of the golden goddess widened. She glanced at L'onee, then at Holroyd. A strange horror crept into her face.

"And don't bother to leave your body to go for help," L'onee said more grimly. "We've got guards stationed in the upper corridors who would admit no one down here except the goddess herself. And they're all men." She broke off, "*Quick,* Ptath, the chains! She's trying to dissolve."

It took a long moment. A mad *thing* clawed at Holroyd's face; and then he had her. Round and round her writhing body he twisted the cold, enveloping chains. There was a sickness in him as L'onee brought the blazing metal link from the forge and he hammered it into place and poured cold water on it to temper it. It was not a good job, but no human muscles would ever break out of it.

Beside him, L'onee said, "Don't be too frightened, my dear. You're to be kept here imprisoned only until Ptath is strong enough to destroy your ability to be a pole of power. Mortal again, you will be allowed to live out your life in peace and comfort. Can you think, Ineznia, of any more fitting punishment?"

"Let's get out of here," Holroyd muttered. "I feel ill."

But it was he who paused at the doorway and stared at the dull-eyed creature in the chains. "You forgot one thing, Ineznia," he said. "The greater the danger, the more mindlessly people sink themselves into their religion; the more ruthlessly your soldiers attempted to make them give up their prayer sticks, the more determinedly they hid them.

"Religion, you see, is not in its roots adoration of a god or a goddess. Religion is fear. Religion is the spark that issues forth when the thought of death or danger strikes the individual. It's personal. It grows out of darkness and uncertainty.

"In the great crisis that you so wantonly created, *what more natural than that women prayed for their soldier husbands and for their loved ones.* They will never regret it, I assure you."

Having spoken, he twisted aside and out through the door where L'onee was waiting. Together, they closed and sealed the door.

Together, they went up out of the darkness toward the light.

The End